ADDITIONAL PRAISE FOR
THE REX GRAVES MYSTERY SERIES

Murder Comes Calling

"Satisfying … Smooth prose will keep cozy fans turning the pages."

—*Publishers Weekly*

"Nicely mixes procedural detail and village charm and will appeal to fans of Deborah Crombie and Anne Cleeland."

—*Booklist*

Murder at Midnight

"A classic country-house mystery, with modern day twists and turns adding to the fun."

—*Booklist*

"What could be better for Agatha Christie whodunit fans than an old-fashioned, Scottish country house murder on New Year's Eve? "

—*Mystery Scene*

"*Murder at Midnight* will delight all cozy and Agatha Christie fans. C. S. creates devilishly complex characters, keeping the reader on edge until the final page … C. S.'s best work to date."

—*Suspense Magazine*

Murder of the Bride

"This is a well-crafted read and a logical and well-plotted conclusion."

—*Crime Fiction Lovers*

Murder on the Moor

"C. S. Challinor delivers a racier cozy in *Murder on the Moor* … skillfully choreographed."

—*Washington Post*

"Contemporary in setting but classic in style and voice, it'll have you guessing to the very end. 4 stars."

—*RT Book Reviews*

"A welcome diversion from today's style of writing … The writing is crisp and the story fast-paced. Challinor doesn't waste time on empty filler, but gets right to the topic at hand."

—*BellaOnline*

Phi Beta Murder

"This is a well-paced mystery that plays fair with the reader and provides a satisfying and surprising conclusion. The writing is crisp and dialogue-driven."

—*Mystery Scene*

"Humor and well-written characters add to the story, as does some reflection on the causes of suicide. A wonderful read and great plot for cozy mystery lovers."

—*ForeWord Reviews*

Murder in the Raw

"*Murder in the Raw* is a clever variant on the locked room mystery. With a host of colorful characters, a dose of humor, and a balmy locale, you will want to devour this well-plotted mystery."

—*Mystery Scene*

"A solid choice for traditional mystery fans, *Murder in the Raw* provides some new twists on something old and familiar."

—*Mystery Reader*

"*Murder in the Raw* is one of the more recent contributions to a growing library of mystery novels of interest to naturists, and naked readers will especially enjoy how Challinor 'gets it right.'"

—*N: Nude and Natural*

Christmas is Murder

*"[A] winner … At times, it seems we are playing Clue or perhaps enjoying a contemporary retelling of a classic Agatha Christie tale *(And Then There Were None,* or *At Bertram's Hotel)* with a charming new sleuth. A must for cozy fans."

—*Booklist* (starred review)

"Challinor's debut is a pleasant modern knockoff of Christie."

—*Kirkus Reviews*

"Graves's next case may be worth watching for."

—*Ellery Queen Mystery Magazine*

"Challinor will keep most readers guessing as she cleverly spreads suspicion and clues that point in one direction, then another."

—*Alfred Hitchcock Mystery Magazine*

"A great start to a new series that is sure to become a modern favorite traditional English cozy series."

—*The Mystery Reader*

"Agatha Christie fans, here you go! You have been waiting for a mystery writer that can hold the torch; well, we found her: C. S. Challinor."

—*Suspense Magazine*

"*Christmas is Murder* is a most enjoyable first mystery in what promises to be a fantastic series. Challinor writes with wit and cheek, and with Rex Graves she has created a thoroughly charming sleuth."

—Rick Miller, host of ABC's
primetime hit series *Just for Laughs*

"C. S. Challinor has crafted a delectable murder mystery set in an old English manor turned hotel. *Christmas is Murder* has all the charm and ambience of a classic Agatha Christie novel. This is mystery at its very best! Challinor is an author to watch. I'll be anxiously awaiting her next book!"

—Nancy Mehl, author of The Ivy Towers Mystery Series

JUDGMENT
— of —
MURDER

A Rex Graves Mystery

JUDGMENT

— of —

MURDER

C. S. CHALLINOR

MIDNIGHT INK

WOODBURY, MINNESOTA

MIDNIGHT
INK

FIRST EDITION
First Printing, 2016

Book format by Bob Gaul
Cover design by Kevin R. Brown
Cover illustration by Dominick Finelle/July Group

Midnight Ink, an imprint of Llewellyn Worldwide Ltd.

Library of Congress Cataloging-in-Publication Data
Names: Challinor, C. S. (Caroline S.), author.
Title: Judgment of murder: a Rex Graves mystery / C. S. Challinor.
Description: Woodbury, Minnesota: Midnight Ink, [2016] | Series: A Rex
   Graves mystery; #8
Identifiers: LCCN 2016026848 (print) | LCCN 2016032125 (ebook) | ISBN
   9780738750095 (softcover) | ISBN 9780738751009 ()
Subjects: LCSH: Graves, Rex (Fictitious character)—Fiction. |
   Murder—Investigation—Fiction. | GSAFD: Mystery fiction.
Classification: LCC PS3603.H3366 J86 2016 (print) | LCC PS3603.H3366 (ebook)
   | DDC 813/.6—dc23
LC record available at https://lccn.loc.gov/2016026848

Midnight Ink
Llewellyn Worldwide Ltd.
2143 Wooddale Drive
Woodbury, MN 55125-2989
www.midnightinkbooks.com

Printed in the United States of America

ACKNOWLEDGMENTS

Special thanks to Joel A. Gonzales, friend and attorney, for setting me straight on a few points of law and other things. Sincere gratitude also to my editor, Sandy Sullivan, for her extraordinary patience and diligence, and for helping keep track of Rex Graves' to-ing and fro-ing between Edinburgh and Canterbury.

Not least, retrospectively, to Connie Hill, for her editorial assistance with past titles. May she be deservedly enjoying her retirement.

~~~

A starless night steeped the lawn and summerhouse in deepening shades of darkness and no lights shone from the residence. A human shape scaled the cast-iron drainpipe, raised the window, and climbed inside, disappearing behind the curtains. An early autumn breeze chased fallen leaves across the path as the distant murmur of traffic dispelled the near silence. Five minutes later, the shadow emerged and made a slow and careful descent down the white stucco wall.

~~~

ONE

Hon. Lord Gordon Murgatroyd QC, 80, passed away peacefully at his home in Canterbury, Kent, early yesterday morning.

REX GRAVES SET THE newspaper down on his desk, leaving his hand resting on the obituaries page. So the old judge had passed away, he mused with a sense of regret. On many an occasion, Rex had prosecuted under his eagle eye at the High Court of Justiciary, Scotland's supreme criminal court, and had found him to be a rather caustic and cantankerous man. Universally considered severe in his sentencing, "Judge Murder" had been Murgatroyd's sobriquet, uttered with trepidation in the halls of justice.

Yet for some reason unknown to Rex, the judge had taken a shine to him, giving him terse pointers and sage advice in the privacy of his chambers.

He left behind a daughter, Phoebe Wells, whom Rex had met a few times in the past. She had moved from Edinburgh when she got married and now lived in Canterbury on the southeast coast of England. Her husband had been a renowned psychiatrist.

1

Rex spent some minutes on the phone locating her number through directory enquiries. Once obtained, he made the dutiful call.

"I don't know if you remember me, Mrs. Wells," he began when she answered. "Rex Graves QC. I wanted to offer my deepest condolences. Your father took me under his wing when I started out and he taught me a lot."

"Of course I remember you! It's so kind of you to ring. Not many of our old acquaintance have, you know." Phoebe Wells spoke in a cultured voice, with the slightest of lisps. "There's to be a small service on Monday. Can you come down?" she asked in the next breath. "My father liked you, and he didn't like many people." She laughed awkwardly. "And, well, I'm troubled, you see."

"Troubled?" Rex repeated in surprise.

"This might sound silly, but ... "

"Go on," Rex prompted.

"Well, it's just that Dad's stamp collection went missing from his room the night he died. And his window wasn't locked. He always kept it shut as he had a phobia about draughts."

Rex attempted to collect his thoughts as Phoebe's words tumbled out in a rush. This was not the conversation he had anticipated having with the bereaved daughter. "I had assumed he died of natural causes," he ventured.

"Presumed heart attack," Phoebe qualified. "Which could have been provoked by shock. I think someone broke into the house and suffocated him. In fact, I'm all but positive that's what happened. I'm glad they put that bit in the paper about him passing away peacefully because I don't want people phoning to enquire, out of morbid curiosity, how exactly he died. I've had newspapers and legal publications requesting interviews as it is. Did you see an obit or did someone tell you?"

"I saw the one in the *Scotsman*." Rex quoted it.

"I always found Dad's titles to be a bit confusing," Phoebe Wells fretted at the other end of the line. "Oh, do say you'll come," she pleaded.

"It's a bit short-notice, I'm afraid," Rex replied. "I'll be in court all next week."

"Oh, I see." Then, after the briefest of pauses, "How about next weekend? It would mean so much to me, and to Dad. I've heard you've had considerable success in solving murders."

Rex sighed inwardly. He had been looking forward to a long-overdue game of golf with his friend and colleague Alistair Frazer. "Are you convinced your father was murdered?" he asked carefully. He could not see an eighty-year-old man being much of a threat to anyone, even if he had been known as Judge Murder.

Phoebe Wells spoke firmly. "I know my father was old, but much as I'd like to believe he died in his sleep, I just can't shake the feeling that something is terribly wrong. My late husband always said to trust one's instincts. Physical feelings, he told me, never lie, and I've been feeling on edge ever since it happened; I don't know—sort of jittery. But I need someone of sound judgement to properly air my suspicions to before I involve the police. I don't want to appear paranoid."

"I'm sure they would not think that. Your father was an eminent jurist." Rex debated with himself for a brief moment. "I'll come," he agreed. He felt he owed it to the old judge. The golf could wait. Murder could not.

TWO

THE FOLLOWING SATURDAY, REX took the early morning train from Edinburgh to London. At St. Pancras he boarded the High Speed Link to Canterbury West Station, which arrived less than an hour later.

With only his weekend bag to carry, and the weather mild and dry that day, he decided to walk to St. Dunstan's Terrace, where Phoebe resided in one of the late Regency townhouses.

Pausing briefly on the pavement, he admired the spacious white residence adorned with grey shutters and a wrought-iron balcony running along the entire upper storey. He mounted the short flight of steps to the varnished red door and rapped on the heavy brass knocker.

A sturdily built woman in a plain black dress and black compression stockings answered the door. Rex was taken aback. Had Phoebe aged so much since he had last seen her ten years ago?

"Mrs. Wells is expecting ye," the elderly woman informed him. "Please come this way."

"Ehm, thank you," he said, instantly disabused of his misconception. This must be the housekeeper. He followed her into the hall where he deposited his bag and removed his coat. "You're from Edinburgh?" he asked. Her accent, thicker than his, was unmistakably Lowland Scots. "Do you get back much?" he enquired.

"Not as much noo."

"And how do you like Canterbury?"

"I like it jist fine." She led him into an elegant drawing room overlooking the quiet residential street.

Phoebe Wells, much as he remembered her, though now with wisps of grey threaded through her mass of dark hair, rose from an armchair. "The tea, Annie," she instructed the older woman, who immediately left the room.

Phoebe welcomed Rex with a soft kiss on the cheek, stretching up on her tiptoes to accomplish the gesture, owing to his above-average stature. "I can't tell you how relieved I am that you accepted my invitation. Have you had lunch?"

Up close, he noticed lines etched around her eyes and downturned mouth, a feature inherited from her father. As was the case with Annie, she wore black, accentuating her natural pallor. The coral lipstick and jade beads around the collar of her turtleneck sweater displayed the only colour on her person.

"A sandwich on the train," he said in reply to her question. "I'm fine. Really."

"Well, Annie will bring us some tea. You look well. In fact, you haven't aged much at all. The same red hair, but perhaps more grizzly in the beard?" Mrs. Wells continued to study him. "It's very distinguished," she pronounced. "And with your height you can carry off a bit of extra weight." She indicated for him to take a chair next to hers.

"How are you?" he asked solicitously, sitting down. "How was the service? I'm sorry to have missed it."

She gave a wan smile. "It was a quiet but dignified send-off. Dad wouldn't have wanted a huge fuss. He's been retired for ten years and has lived most of them here, largely forgotten by everyone back home in Edinburgh."

Rex privately disputed the notion of his being forgotten. Judge Murder was something of a legend in Scottish legal circles and often talked about, especially since his death. An American colleague had referred to him wryly as His Orneryness. Lord Murgatroyd may have been avoided by some after his retirement, but never forgotten.

"Dad became something of a recluse," Phoebe went on, fingering her jade necklace. "He couldn't go out by himself towards the end as he tended to wander about and get lost."

Rex nodded in commiseration.

"In any case, it wasn't safe for him to be out on his own. An old man was robbed and beaten to death on St. Dunstan's Terrace shortly before Dad died." Phoebe gave an uncomprehending sigh.

"Was the mugger caught?"

She shook her head. "I don't think there were any eyewitnesses, otherwise the police would have released one of those composite sketches. I expect it was some yob looking for drug money. Anyway, the point is I couldn't think who to invite to the funeral. But I bought Dad the very best coffin. Solid oak with beautiful brass fittings." Phoebe blinked away tears and looked down at the pale, manicured hands clasped in her lap.

"Ye did him proud," Annie remarked, bustling in with a tea tray, which she placed on the low table between the two occupied armchairs.

"Thank you, Annie. I'll take care of this. She's a wonder in the kitchen," Phoebe confided to Rex when the housekeeper had left the room. "Especially in the baking department. Please help yourself to a scone," she said as she poured the tea.

"How many years has Annie been in your employ?" Rex asked, splitting open a scone still warm from the oven. He helped himself to butter and strawberry jam.

"Two years. Before that I had a live-in student who attended the university. Michaela. She was supposed to help with Dad in return for free board, but she wasn't very reliable. Annie came highly recommended by the family she charred for in Edinburgh. She had just lost her husband and wanted to move south to be closer to her daughter and grandchildren in Essex. In a place called Brightlingsea."

"Never heard of it." Rex munched into his scone.

"It's a small coastal town. London day trippers own most of the beach huts along the shore, or at least they did when I was last there. But that was a long time ago, with my husband."

"I was sorry to hear aboot Dr. Wells," Rex said with grave sincerity. He had found him to be an astute and agreeable man on the few occasions he had met him socially in Edinburgh.

"His death was so sudden." Phoebe sighed heavily as she restored her tea cup to its saucer on the table.

"I forget the circumstances," Rex faltered in apology.

"An aneurism. It happened while he was preparing oysters for a party. I can't bear to look at an oyster now. You never remarried, did you?"

"I'm engaged, as a matter of fact." Rex smiled at the thought of Helen.

"Oh." Phoebe stiffened in her chair. "How nice," she added belatedly.

"So you still have doubts regarding your father's death," Rex stated, since that was the main purpose of his visit.

"Yes, and more so than ever. You don't think I'm being irrational, do you? Dad wasn't always an easy man to get along with, especially during the last years of his life, but I hate the thought of him suffering at some evil person's hand and never knowing the truth."

"Do you fear the killer might come back?" Rex asked with concern for her safety.

Phoebe shook her head in the negative, and then paused. "Well, I suppose I do in a way, although that's not what's been preying on my mind. I mean, wouldn't I have been murdered at the same time if that was the intruder's intention?"

"You were home that night?"

"I'm almost always home," she said bitterly.

Rex feared this might be a long weekend and began to privately question Phoebe Wells' motives for inviting him to Canterbury. Hopefully, her account of foul play was not pure fabrication.

An unlocked window and a missing stamp album were not a lot to be going on with, he reflected. The story about the old man being mugged in the street would have to be verified. In the meantime, he had little choice but to continue with his investigation and hope either to catch the killer or else catch Phoebe out in a lie.

THREE

Rex fortified himself with more tea. "And your housekeeper?" he pursued, accepting another scone. "Was she also home the night your father passed away?"

"Wednesday is her night off," Phoebe replied, setting down her teacup. "She went to the cinema with a friend from her Presbyterian church and stayed over at the woman's house. I checked in on Dad before going to bed. He usually turned in by nine with his mug of Horlicks."

"He was awake?"

"Sound asleep, and so I switched off his reading lamp. The coroner estimated his death as occurring in the early hours of the morning. He hadn't seen his own doctor in over two weeks. That was for angina, and the nitroglycerine medication seemed to be working. I'm sure his condition was what led the coroner to conclude he had a heart attack."

"You say a stamp album went missing. Anything else?" Rex looked about him. The drawing room was full of portable antiques and valuables, ripe for the picking.

"Dad's watch," Phoebe replied. "I mean, I can't be sure since he was always misplacing things, but I haven't been able to find it. I turned the house upside down again before you arrived. It should have been on his bedside table. It was the last thing he removed after his spectacles. Dad was obsessed with time."

Rex recalled what a stickler for punctuality the judge had been in his courtroom. "What sort of watch was it?"

"A gold-plated wristwatch. A good Swiss make, but nothing fancy. The face was scratched, and I kept meaning to get it replaced. It had large numbers he could read."

Rex stretched out his legs, crossing them at the ankles. "Tell me aboot the stamp collection."

"Well," Phoebe began slowly. "He kept it on his desk. He was still working on it. He had a filled album in one of the drawers. The lock wasn't forced and that album wasn't taken."

"Was the one you think was stolen worth anything?"

Phoebe shrugged. "I know next to nothing about stamps. But it's not as though he had a Penny Black, or anything like that. He would have told me if he had. The main attraction for him, I think, were the exotic places of origin and the appealing designs. A lot of them, though, looked very ordinary. He visited a local dealer from time to time before he became housebound."

"Perhaps I could take a look at the completed album later, not that stamps are my thing either. And perhaps you could give me the name of the dealer to follow up on. Now, what aboot a will? Any incentive for murder there?"

"Dad left everything to me. There was no one else. And my late husband was well-off. Titled, you know. An old Welsh family. Anyway, I'm not sure what I'm going to do with all that money. Not to sound ungrateful." Phoebe Wells made a rueful face. "It's just that I never had any children, nor even nieces or nephews. So I've been looking into charities."

Rex decided he had mined Phoebe for sufficient information for the time being. He needed to get another perspective on the business of the judge's alleged murder. "I'll take the tea tray to the kitchen and save Annie a trip," he said, pushing himself out of the armchair.

"How thoughtful of you. She is getting on a bit." Phoebe stacked the crockery on the tray. "The kitchen is in the basement."

"Your housekeeper knows nothing of your suspicions?"

"Lord no. Not until I can be certain. I don't want to frighten the poor woman off."

"What is Annie's surname?"

"McBride." Phoebe rose to open the double doors leading into the hall, and Rex carried the tray through them and down the stairs.

At the bottom he found a large kitchen housing a blue Aga with a backsplash of antique Dutch tiles. Annie stood at the porcelain sink, hands immersed in sudsy water washing a pile of cooking utensils, even though there was what appeared to be a perfectly serviceable dishwasher under the counter.

Startled by his presence, she glanced over her shoulder. Rex deduced she must be a bit deaf not to have heard him enter with a tray of rattling crockery. He wasn't the most adept waiter in the world.

"Just leave it there," she replied, nodding towards the counter, and thanked him for bringing it down.

"There are a great many stairs in this house," he sympathized. "It must involve a lot of work."

"It's hard on the legs." The black stockings failed to conceal the housekeeper's prominent varicose veins. "But it's a grand auld hoose, and Mrs. Wells doesna entertain much, so it's no that taxing, especially since her father left us."

11

"How was he to work for?"

"Didna have much to say for hisself. Did for hisself mostly, but he took breakfast and lunch in his room. It was too tiring for him to be going up and doon the stairs, so I helped wi' the fetching and carrying."

Rex wondered if she would stay on now. "You live in, I take it?"

"Aye, there's a suite doon here for my use."

Rex noticed a small seating area off the kitchen and a portable television on a shelf, switched on to the news. An anchor woman was reporting the disappearance of a fourteen-year-old girl in Kent, last seen walking home from school on Thursday. The landmark white cliffs of Dover loomed into view, not all that imposing in reality, as Rex recalled from a trip across the Channel to Calais. A photo of a smiling young face framed with long, light brown hair followed on the screen. The Port of Dover Police had launched an extensive search after a suspicious-looking transit van had been seen near the girl's school.

"Mrs. Wells tells me you have family in Essex," Rex said conversationally, turning back to the housekeeper. He really wanted to ask her about the mugging of the old man, but could not see how to broach the subject without appearing macabre.

"Aye, I plan on moving in wi' my daughter and her three girls upon retirement, which is coming up."

Rex leaned against the counter while Annie busied herself with scrubbing a colander. Her profile beneath the wiry grey hair presented a low forehead sloping to a button nose and a pursed mouth that all but disappeared in a pucker of wrinkles. A loose chin hung to her throat.

"You'll be sorely missed," he said. "Mrs. Wells speaks very highly of you."

"I'm pleased to hear that," Annie said without looking up from the sink.

He felt he would not get much else out of the housekeeper, who probably wondered what business any of this was of his. After all, she didn't know he was supposed to be investigating a murder. He left her to her chores and re-joined Phoebe in the drawing room just as she was ending a phone call.

"That was Andrew Doyle, a former clerk of court in Edinburgh, calling to see how I was. Such a sweet old dear."

"The name rings a bell. He must be retired now. Talking of retirement, Annie says she'll be leaving you soon."

Phoebe sighed in mild frustration. "I'll have to find someone else or sell this place. It's really far too big for me." She put her hand to her temple. "I think I'll lie down, if you don't mind. Will you be all right? Let me show you to your room first so you can settle in. Just come and go as you please and make yourself at home."

"Thank you. I'll see if I can talk to the stamp dealer. May I take the finished album to show him?"

"Of course. I'd be curious to see if it's worth anything." Phoebe led Rex upstairs, explaining on the way that her father had slept at the opposite end of the house from her front-facing bedroom, and consequently she had not heard anything the night of his death. "However," she added, "I am a light sleeper, so the intruder must have been very quiet. I suppose that's why they're called cat burglars."

Rex paused on the landing. "Going back to the old man who was mugged…"

Phoebe turned to face him. "Mr. Rogers. Yes?"

"You don't see a connection with your father's death?"

"Not really. They're so different. I mean, Dad's murderer had to have been a professional to get in and out without being noticed, don't you think?"

Rex pondered Phoebe's reasoning. Perhaps her murderer had just been lucky. Or perhaps he didn't exist at all, except in her own mind.

FOUR

Rex stood leafing through a moleskin-covered album entitled "Worldwide" on the inside page in green ink, written in the judge's distinctive curlicue longhand. Multicolour postage stamps of different shapes and currencies swelled the gridded pages arranged by country of origin, everywhere from Norway and Spain to the Sudan and minor republics. Postmarked images of ships, astronauts, birds, buildings, and flags were interspersed with mint commemorative sets of topical themes and religious scenes.

By far the largest number of stamps featured Queen Elizabeth II's crowned head in various muted shades assembled under Great Britain and its Commonwealth Realms. Some preceded her long reign. A few looked to be quite old, but how rare, Rex could not tell.

Had the alleged murderer been seeking valuable stamps, unaware that the completed album was secreted in the locked drawer of the desk, or had he found what he was looking for in the unfinished collection lying on top? Rex hoped the dealer would be able to shed some light on the matter.

The missing album had left a large space in the centre of the desk. On the periphery remained a soaking bowl, a magnifying glass, miniature tongs, and a box containing a jumble of small glassine envelopes, first-day covers, and packets of adhesive hinges.

"Where did he procure the stamps?" he asked Phoebe who was quietly watching while he examined the items.

"He sent off for them, mostly, and he attended stamp auctions. My husband received international mail from his book publications and saved the envelopes for him. Dad wasn't at his collection all the time. It was more of a hobby than an investment, I think. He also liked to compile crossword puzzles for the *Canterbury Tales*, a weekly newsletter for retirees. It helped occupy his time and kept his brain active."

Inserted among the reference works on philately and stamp catalogues stacked beneath an angle-poise reading lamp lay a hardcover *Oxford English Dictionary*. Law books lined the surrounding shelves.

"Anybody at the newsletter I should talk to?" Rex queried, turning towards Phoebe and resting a hand on the back of the brown leather chair in front of the desk.

"I don't think he ever met the editor in person. They talked on the phone, and Dad sent his crosswords by post. He'd use a theme connected with Canterbury, like Chaucer, for instance. I could never finish one. Far too erudite for me. A small prize was awarded for the first correct entry, usually a book on local history." Phoebe sighed. Rex had noticed she did that a lot. "Not sure what I'll do with this room now," she announced. "Perhaps keep it as a library. Would you like any of the books? I'm sure Dad would have wanted you to have some."

She walked towards the large sash window across from the desk. "I could turn it into a sewing room as it gets decent light, but I don't do much dress-making these days."

The multi-paned window, draped and valanced in russet brown velvet, took in a view of the rear garden. As Rex approached, his gaze alighted upon a hexagonal whitewood summerhouse in the middle of the lawn, with what looked to be a gold-painted pineapple atop its cupola.

"The summerhouse was there when we bought the property," Phoebe explained beside him. "It has wooden benches built into the six walls. I put cushions inside when the weather's nice so I can sit out and read. You should see it when it's surrounded by roses."

Rex could picture the delightful setting. No doubt the view was one of the reasons the judge had taken this room. His eye followed a crazy-paving path through the flowerbeds, shrubs, and silver birch trees to a separate garage. He supposed the garages had replaced the coach-houses originally built for the affluent terrace of homes. "Is that gate by the garage kept locked?" he asked.

"Yes, but anyone halfway fit could get over it. It leads to New Street. The intruder must have climbed the drainpipe to gain access to this room. I would have notified the police, but I thought they'd only think I was overreacting from grief. And quite frankly I didn't relish the idea of them traipsing all over the house and poking around until I was quite sure the watch and album weren't lying around somewhere. Dad would lose things in the strangest places."

"My mother does the same thing with her keys and her knitting; puts them down and then forgets where." Rex pulled back the iron catch on the window frame and pushed up the lower panel, which opened with relative ease and only a faint squeak. Sniffing the metal tracks, he was unable to detect any distinct odour of lubricant. "When was this last oiled?"

"My handyman takes care of all that, but I haven't had to call him in a year. He's been coming since before my husband died.

Doug couldn't put up a shelf to save his life and he never had the right tools. He said it wasn't worth his time fiddling around with that sort of thing when an expert could do it in half the time."

"What is the name of your handyman?"

"Alan Burke."

Rex could find no suspicious gouges or scratches on the windowsill or frames. Old defects had been painted over. No evidence of fingerprints existed, at least none visible to the naked eye. However, a professional housebreaker would have worn gloves, he reflected.

"Has the room been cleaned since your father passed away?"

"Annie came in and did a thorough clean and airing."

The queen-size bed, flanked by matching antique nightstands and shade lamps, had been stripped. A copy of *Bleak House* missing a dust jacket sat on the near-side table, a yellow silk ribbon separating half the thick block of pages. The judge's spectacles were still folded on top of the cover.

If the housekeeper had cleaned thoroughly enough, any clues would have been eliminated; an unfortunate state of affairs, in the event the police were called.

"Did you check the window that night?"

"I didn't think to. The curtains were drawn, and, anyway, Dad never opened the window, and that particular night it was damp and cold. I only discovered it was unlocked the next morning."

"And the exterior doors?"

"They're fitted with alarms."

Rex tried to imagine what the old man would have thought upon finding a stranger in his room. If indeed it was a stranger. Possibly he had not had much time to react. "Any dogs in the neighbourhood that might have been heard barking in the night?" he asked. He knew he was grasping at straws. Over a week had passed since the judge's death, and he doubted any of the neighbours would remember a disturbance in the wee hours.

She thought for a moment. "There's a dachshund at the far end of the street, but I never hear it."

"Any sensory lights?" Rex asked, peering out again into the garden.

"Just a security light by the garage. It's not very bright."

"I'll take a look when I go down. Have you had much rain this past week?"

Phoebe nodded. "A fair amount."

She looked tired and drawn, and sounded weary. Rex told her he would get on with his investigation and let her rest. She nodded gratefully and took off to her room, saying she would see him later.

He stopped by the guest suite he had been allocated at the top of the stairs and exchanged his shirt for a cashmere sweater to wear beneath his tweed jacket. He planned to walk to the stamp dealer's shop and take in the cathedral and the ruins of the Norman castle while he was about it. In the event he was on a wild goose chase, he thought he might as well do some sightseeing and make the most of his sabotaged weekend.

FIVE

At the bottom of High Street by the bridge over the River Great Stour stood Westgate, a turreted medieval gatehouse sixty feet high built of Kentish rag stone, the last of seven once posted around the city. Motorised traffic now passed in steady procession under the arch between its drum towers. On a weekday Rex imagined the road became rather congested.

The weather had continued mild, though cloudy, well into the afternoon, and he strolled up the semi-pedestrianised street among the Saturday shoppers and tourists, thinking how nice it would have been to be taking in the historic sites with Helen. A group of Americans had paused in front of the ornately fronted Caffè Nero where, the guide was explaining, Queen Elizabeth I had stayed in 1573 when it was the Crown Inn.

Minutes later, Rex came across a narrow shopfront with "Stamps & Collectibles" scrolled in black lettering on the glass. Chock-full of antiques and curios, it conjured up a distinctly Dickensian feel, an impression reinforced when he stepped inside and saw a diminutive man behind the counter dressed in a black waistcoat and jacket and bearing the sombre and solicitous air of an undertaker.

"Good day to you," he greeted Rex, his grey face set in an expression of helpful enquiry, one immobile eye fixed at nothing in particular while the other regarded his visitor.

"You are Christopher Penn, the owner?" Rex enquired, towering over him.

The man nodded and smiled without parting his thin bloodless lips.

"I'm a colleague of the late Gordon Murgatroyd." Rex placed his business card on the mahogany counter. "I believe you were acquainted with the judge?"

"Indeed, sir. And sympathies." Elbows propped on the counter, Penn raised folded hands to his chin. "I'd not seen him in a long while. I sent his daughter a condolence card when I heard the sad news. I would have sent flowers, but they were expressly discouraged." He smiled sorrowfully. "What can I do for you?"

Rex removed the stamp album from the canvas shopping bag lent him by Annie before he went out on his excursion. "His daughter, Mrs. Wells, is interested in a quick evaluation of his collection." He set the album down on the counter. "I thought I'd bring it in and get your professional opinion, if you'd be so kind."

Penn hummed and hawed as he turned the stamp-laden pages, occasionally peering through a magnifier, using his good eye. Rex could not help but observe that he had long, translucent fingers resembling tentacles. Rather than stare, compelling as the man's appearance was, he looked about him at the wares crammed and stacked on shelves and cubby holes against the walls. A musty whiff of mildew pervaded the cluttered space, and he imagined years of accumulated dust lurking in every corner and crevice.

"None of these are mounted," the dealer murmured, calling back Rex's attention.

"Is there anything a layman like myself would miss, an imperfection that would increase the value of a stamp, perhaps?"

"Not that I can see." Penn's right eye looked downwards while the glass one gazed ahead disconcertingly at Rex's midsection. "Judge Murgatroyd was an amateur philatelist." He stressed the word "amateur" with mild disdain. "These Victorian ones are nicely preserved, but not all that rare. The collection is a bit of a hodge-podge, to be honest. We have here an almost complete floral set of Hungarians from the mid to late twentieth century, but almost is the operative word. Hmm ... This one from India might conceivably sell for twenty euros shopped to the right buyer ... "

Nothing worth murdering for so far, it seemed. Rex waited while the dealer completed his inspection and mumbled the occasional observation, much of it lost upon him.

"It's a nice collection," Penn said at last, closing the album. "But I personally wouldn't offer more than two hundred pounds for the lot. If Mrs. Wells has the time and inclination, she could try selling individual items on eBay, to someone, say, interested in expanding their Egyptian or Japanese collection. If you'd care to leave this with me, I could possibly select a few to buy on my clients' account?"

"I'm not sure she wishes to sell the album or else break it up," Rex demurred, not feeling at liberty to leave the un-inventoried collection in the dealer's hands.

Penn nodded. "Quite. It may well hold sentimental value for her."

"Mrs. Wells may also have wanted to know how much to insure it for, had it been worth doing. But thank you, Mr. Penn. I very much appreciate your time, and I'll pass on your comments."

The doorbell chimed, and a young couple entered the shop and began browsing among the oil lamps and hand-painted crockery and old silver spoons piled upon pine chests and sagging gateleg tables. Rex packed up the album and thanked the dealer again for his time.

On his way out, he stopped to examine a rack of gilt-framed engravings of the city. He decided to purchase one that highlighted the medieval grandeur of Canterbury Cathedral as a gift for his mother. He returned to the counter and discovered Mr. Penn to be a wealth of information on its history, distracting as his blind eye was as he was giving his fascinating discourse.

All the more inspired to see where Archbishop Thomas Becket had been slain by four of Henry II's sword-wielding knights, Rex made his way to the cathedral, while pondering his own case of murder. It appeared the album held nothing of significant value, and the retired high court judge had pursued stamp collecting solely as a pastime, with no view to making money out of it. So why had the other been stolen?

All he had was Phoebe's assertion that the album had in fact been stolen, along with the watch. A close look in the garden before he had left her house had revealed nothing suspicious around the old cast-iron drainpipe by the window or at the surmountable gate next to the garage. The judge, despite his phobia about draughts, might have simply taken it into his head to open the window that night, however inclement the weather, and forgotten to lock it.

And yet, another old man had been mugged in the same street. A strange sequence of events, perhaps, but did it amount to murder?

SIX

WHEN REX RETURNED TO St. Dunstan's Terrace almost two hours later, he was no more convinced there was enough evidence to hang a murder on than before. Failing to encounter Phoebe on the main floor, he went down to the basement kitchen to return the carrier bag to her housekeeper.

Annie was spooning loose black tea into a pot on the counter. The tantalizing aroma of a casserole wafted from the Aga. Rex suddenly realized how hungry he was after his walk around town.

"Will ye be wanting a cup of tea?" she asked.

"Gladly." He watched as she strained the tea into an enamel mug embossed with a gold coat of arms, no doubt that of Phoebe's late husband's family. "I've been walking around Canterbury," he told her in a casual tone. "St. Dunstan's Terrace is a grand location, central and yet quiet. Though Mrs. Wells mentioned a local resident was mugged here recently?"

"Dinna fear." Annie took in his height and breadth. "You could take two of them muggers on."

"Were you acquainted with the victim?"

"Noo."

"What time of day did it happen?" he asked in gossipy fashion, enhancing his Scots accent for her benefit.

"Early evening, I think they said on the news. One or two louts taking advantage of a pensioner. I dinna ken more than that."

"An opportunistic attack, by all accounts." Rex shook his head perplexedly and helped himself to the milk and sugar the house-keeper put in front of him.

He thanked her for the tea and took the mug upstairs where he found Phoebe in the drawing room plumping up the sofa cushions. "I would have brought you some tea if I'd known you had come down," he said. "Did you have a good rest?"

"Wonderful and just what I needed. Thank you, but I think I'll have some wine." She crossed to a custom-built drinks cabinet, where a panelled door concealed a mini-fridge, and retrieved a bottle of Venezie Pinot Grigio.

He declined the glass she offered. "I was asking Annie aboot the mugging, but she could not tell me much." He joined Phoebe on the capacious sofa. "Did you know the old man?"

"Only slightly. He was a retired chartered accountant. He came to the house a few times to play chess with Dad. But having a conversation with Albert was a challenge because he was rather deaf, in spite of his hearing aid. He lived with his sister Elspeth three doors down. I didn't tell Dad what happened to Albert. It would only have upset him. And then he passed away himself a few days later. Do you actually think there might be a connection?"

"I would not discount it." Rex did not add: "If your father did not die of natural causes." He went on, "Two attacks on retired men in the space of a few days makes me wonder, especially in light of the unlocked window and the missing watch and album. Taken together, the incidents assume greater significance, even if I am at a loss as to who might have perpetrated the crimes."

Phoebe nodded, apparently satisfied with his analysis. With nothing left to glean about the mugging, he proceeded to tell her about his outing in town and what the stamp dealer had told him.

"No, I'm not interested in selling," she confirmed when she heard Christopher Penn's offer. "Perhaps I can continue the collection in my dotage." Her laugh sounded hollow to Rex's ears.

"You could start now," he suggested, thinking it might be good for her to have another interest, although he didn't really know how she spent her time. "It might help you feel close to your father, and you might meet some interesting people. On the subject of interesting people, Mr. Penn is a curious individual. Have you ever met him?"

Phoebe shook her head.

"He takes stamp collecting very seriously, naturally enough, not that I saw any stamps on display at his shop, and he appears to regard those who dabble in it with mild contempt."

"Collectors can be snobs that way. They think you can't appreciate things unless you're an expert. I'm assuming Mr. Penn is one of those people?"

"A nice man, but a wee bit, well, I hesitate to say sinister, because he's not, really. I suppose his false eye contributes to that regrettable impression. I can't help but think he could possibly get a better one nowadays."

"He lost it as a boy, Dad told me. An older boy accidentally shot him in the woods with a BB gun. I don't know why he wouldn't get a new eye. An optician told me you have to take them out to clean them." Phoebe shuddered.

"At any rate, you should get a second opinion regarding the album's value to ensure Penn's appraisal is unbiased."

"I could take it to an expert in London. Now, I don't want your weekend to be all about work!"

Rex smiled and said if the weather was nice the next day, they could visit Westgate Gardens and get a pub lunch.

Phoebe's face lit up at the suggestion. "Yes, I'd like that. I haven't been in ages, and the Gardens are still pretty at this time of year. We could go punting if the weather holds up."

Annie came to tell them dinner was ready, and they repaired to the formal dining room.

Rex looked about him. "Dining in style, I see."

A crystal chandelier dangled from a crown medallion of white plaster above the oval mahogany table. Murals depicting Dionysus wreathed in vine leaves and frolicking with a bevy of nymphs lent an appropriate backdrop to entertaining. Phoebe explained that her late husband had engaged an artist to paint the scenes from a collection of ancient Greek urns.

"I think they came out rather well," she said, contemplating the figures in ochre relief on the walls. "Doug had excellent taste. I daren't change a thing in the house and spoil the effect."

"It's a most elegant and yet comfortable home," Rex agreed.

Two place settings had been laid at one end of the table. In the centre, a decanter of red wine waited by the silver salt and pepper shakers in a matching antique cruet. Rex did the honours and raised his glass to his hostess. Phoebe went on to tell him about other *objets d'art* she and her husband had brought back from their travels. Only when they were half way through the meal did the conversation return to Judge Murgatroyd and his, in Phoebe's words, suspicious death.

"I think there must be more to Dad's murder than a random burglary," she said.

Rex refilled their wine glasses. "When I get back to Edinburgh, I'll ask Mr. Doyle, the former clerk of court, if he remembers anyone from your father's past who might have held a grudge. But after all these years it's a long shot," he cautioned. "Your father hadn't presided in court in over a decade."

"But he did have a reputation for being severe in his rulings. He used to tell me, 'Why should the buggers get off lightly when they didn't show the same consideration for their victims?'"

Rex chuckled and dabbed at his mouth with his linen napkin. "That certainly sounds like him."

"But Dad was fair. There was an accused man, his name was *P* something." Phoebe furrowed her brow. "It's on the tip of my tongue. So frustrating! It'll probably come back to me at four in the morning. Anyway, the jury on this particular case was all but deadlocked. The man was accused of assaulting a young girl and dumping her body in Skinner's Close. The very name of the place makes me shiver."

Skinner's Close in Edinburgh, one of several dark passages tucked between grey stone tenements and serving as shortcuts from one part of the Old Town to the other, had become notorious after the murder. "I remember," Rex said. "His name was Pruitt. Richard Pruitt."

It was a name no one acquainted with the case could easily forget.

SEVEN

"THAT'S RIGHT," PHOEBE EXCLAIMED. "Well done! I knew his name began with a 'P.'"

"I recall the public outcry when the verdict came in 'not proven.'"

Scottish law allowed for three verdicts: Guilty, not guilty, or not proven. Not proven applied where the evidence was deemed insufficient to convict beyond reasonable doubt and yet sufficient to suppose the accused might be guilty.

"Nobody thought Richard Pruitt should go free, but Dad managed to convey to the jury that an outright conviction was not a fair verdict in his case."

"That's not strictly the purview of a judge," Rex countered with a smile.

"Well, the police never found the murder weapon, or the second witness, and there wasn't enough DNA. Richard Pruitt sent Dad a postage stamp as a token of gratitude and they kept in touch."

"And your dad accepted the stamp?" Rex asked in surprise. Judges had to be careful about receiving gifts that might be construed as bribes. However, Judge Murgatroyd had been about to retire to the relief of many at court and perhaps not overly concerned about allegations of corruption.

"It wasn't a valuable stamp, I don't think," Phoebe explained in her father's defence. "And it was after the verdict was reached. Mr. Pruitt collected stamps and must have found out about Dad's interest in them. It was an American stamp representing the scales of justice. Dad was quite pleased with it." She shook her head, smiling. "I'd forgotten all about that stamp. I wonder if it's still in the album."

Rex thought for a moment. He had looked at many stamps that afternoon and this one did not stand out in his memory. "We could take another gander."

"He lives in Ramsay Garden. Pruitt, I mean. You wouldn't expect a killer to live at such a smart Edinburgh address, would you? But that's silly of me," Phoebe said, coming back on her question. "Monsters can live anywhere, and do."

"Pruitt wasn't found guilty," Rex reminded her. "I know Ramsay Garden quite well. Perhaps I can pay him a visit." After all, Pruitt was one of the few people who had continued to have contact with Phoebe's father after the judge retired.

Annie placed a platter of cheeses and a tin of crackers on the table and made her exit again after enquiring if they would like coffee. Rex helped himself to a wedge of Blue Stilton.

"Richard Pruitt continued to protest his innocence to Dad," Phoebe said. "He even had a theory about who was responsible for the girl's death."

Rex found the stamp connection interesting, but more anecdotal than helpful in the matter at hand—that of the judge's possible murder. After all, Pruitt was indebted to the old man, and therefore not a likely suspect. He suggested to Phoebe a more practical approach.

"You could always report the watch and album missing to the police. No need to say you suspect murder at this point, just theft."

Phoebe reflected as she took a sip of wine. "I'd rather have more to go on. Not sure they'd be very interested in an old watch and an unfinished stamp collection."

"But what if the watch should turn up in a pawn shop? Or someone tries to sell the stamps? Then we'd know who was in the house." If someone was, he mused.

"I hadn't thought of that. Dad's name was engraved on the back of the watch face, so it would be easy to trace." Phoebe became more animated. "It was a present from my mum on their tenth wedding anniversary. That's why he cherished it."

She paused and gazed wonderingly at Rex. "Dad hasn't been buried long. Do you think we could have his body exhumed in case the coroner missed a vital clue, not knowing Dad might have been murdered? I know one shouldn't disturb the dead, but my father didn't believe in the Hereafter. He was very pragmatic and would have wanted us to bring the perpetrator to justice."

"I hope an exhumation won't be necessary," Rex faltered, appalled at the thought of unearthing the old man's remains. He was surprised Phoebe should even suggest it. How close had she really been to her father? And yet she appeared to feel deeply about finding the culprit in his alleged murder. Perhaps it was the wine talking. His hostess was on her third glass and proved to be a little tipsy when she rose from the table. He helped her upstairs to her father's old room.

Once there, he switched on the desk lamp and put on his reading glasses. They perused the album again and found Pruitt's stamp in the United States section inconspicuously aligned among an assortment of postage depicting variously hued presidents' heads and famous landmarks. The stamp in question was a vertical rectangle in ultramarine with a perforated edge, issued in 1961 and costing four cents at the time, in pristine condition and bearing no discernible water or franking marks. Rex peeled off the folded transparent hinge and inspected the reverse side, which proved blank. Everything in this case was coming up blank, he all but despaired, replacing the stamp and crossing to the large sash window.

He parted the russet panels and looked out, just as a hard, bright moon slid behind a scalloped bank of clouds, eclipsing the garden in pitch black. He gave a sudden start when Phoebe touched his arm. Deep in thought, he had not heard or sensed her approach while he gazed towards the faint light by the back gate.

"A penny for them," she said softly.

After locking the album up in the drawer, she enticed him back downstairs with the offer of a nightcap, saying she had a bottle of Glenlivet which she remembered he liked. She helped herself to some whisky at the drinks cabinet and brought the cut-glass tumblers to the sofa.

"This is a rare treat," Rex thanked her. "And dinner was grand. I'll be sure to thank Annie."

"She's a treasure." Phoebe's lisp had become more pronounced. "I never was much of a cook. Doug was in his element in the kitchen. It's one of the many things I miss about him."

After some desultory conversation, Phoebe asked if he would like to watch the news, and he readily agreed. There had been enough conversation, and he was beginning to feel tired after his day of travel and sightseeing. She retrieved the remote from the coffee table and clicked on the television encased in a mahogany entertainment unit. A recognizable face appeared on the screen, but Rex couldn't place it at first. From the commentary, he quickly realized it belonged to the girl who had gone missing in Dover, whom he had first heard about in Phoebe's kitchen that afternoon.

Much was made of the fact that Lindsay Poulson was a model pupil and a gifted flute player, popular and fun-loving. She was happy at home and had no reason to run away, an aunt told a reporter. If the girl had been abducted, could the culprit now be in France? The talking heads discussed this possibility. And, if so, what had he done with the girl? The grieving parents and grandparents made appeals to the abductor, and the police to the public. Five foot-two, slender build, light brown hair and blue eyes, with a mole on her left cheekbone. Had anyone seen her?

"Heart-breaking," Phoebe said with a sigh, muting the sound on the television. "Almost makes me glad I don't have daughters to worry about. Nor do you. Is it me, or are child abductions getting more frequent?"

"I've been dealing with more crimes against minors," Rex allowed. "Both girls and boys. They're by far the most troubling."

"What is *wrong* with people who intentionally hurt children?" Phoebe deplored, lifting the tumbler to her lips. She swallowed the remaining whisky and slumped back against the beige kidskin sofa, arms akimbo.

Rex hoped he would not have to help her to bed. He was wary of inebriated women, especially those in an emotionally vulnerable state. Her head lolled towards him on the padded backrest and she gazed into his eyes with her mouth partly open. Some of her lipstick had rubbed off and smeared the rim of her glass.

Fortunately for him, Annie interrupted the moment by knocking on the open door and approached the sofa. "Dinner is all cleared away, Mrs. Wells. Will there be anything else?" She stood with her roughened red hands clasped at the front of her white apron. "Can I turn down the bed for ye?"

Phoebe raised her fingers in a gesture of kind dismissal, but Rex jumped in, saying, "I was just going to bed myself. Why don't we both escort Mrs. Wells upstairs?"

Annie caught on quickly and leaned forward to take Phoebe's arm under the elbow. "Up ye come," she said in a gentle yet no-nonsense tone. Evidently this wasn't the first time her employer had been in need of assistance up the stairs. Rex took Phoebe's other arm, but hung back at the bannister, which she managed to hold on to while Annie walked up beside her. The housekeeper was wheezing by the time they reached the landing.

Rex bid his hostess good night and thanked Annie for the wonderful beef casserole; privately thanking her also for saving him from a potentially awkward situation on the downstairs sofa.

He climbed the next flight of stairs to his room, keenly aware of a few aching joints. The guest bathroom featured a claw-foot Victorian tub, which he decided to take advantage of before retiring to bed. The following morning he would take Phoebe to enjoy the river charms of Westgate Gardens and then catch the train back to London after lunch. He felt he had done as much as he could in Canterbury. Investigating a doubtful murder was one thing; comforting a lonely, grief-stricken woman who might have designs on him was another quandary entirely.

EIGHT

THE NEXT DAY, REX was finishing up breakfast in the dining room when Phoebe joined him. She had discarded her dark mourning clothes of the previous day and wore a mint green pullover and soft brown slacks, which enlivened her whole appearance.

"I hope you slept well," she said cheerfully as she sat down at her place mat opposite his at the oval mahogany table.

"I did," Rex replied, folding the newspaper whose front page featured further details on Lindsay Poulson's disappearance. "And I partook of your grand old bath."

"Doug loved Victoriana, as you've probably noticed. This," Phoebe said, reaching back to the sideboard, "is a Victorian nutcracker. Isn't it fun?" She held up an iron crocodile whose jaws clamped shut when she opened its split tail. "The dining room is a bit formal for breakfast, but it was either here or the kitchen. I usually breakfast in my room."

Rex took a bite of buttered toast. "No complaints here."

She smiled sheepishly at him. "Sorry I got a bit wobbly last night. The Glenlivet went straight to my head! I'm not used to it."

He waved aside her apology. "As long as you have no after-effects this morning."

"Right as rain," she pronounced.

Annie entered the dining room and asked what Mrs. Wells would like for breakfast. Phoebe said she would have her usual muesli and fruit. Rex declined more toast. He had eaten two soft-boiled eggs and three crispy rashes of bacon and was well content.

"Have you been up long?" Phoebe asked him as Annie cleared his plate.

"Since eight. I managed to complete your father's crossword in the *Canterbury Tales* newsletter I found in my room."

"Clever you!"

"I would have had more difficulty had I not visited the cathedral yesterday and refreshed my knowledge of its history. There were a lot of medieval references and obscure clues relating to Thomas Becket and the Plantagenet kings that had me stumped for a while."

"Henry the Second turned on Becket for being too big for his boots," Phoebe said. "But at least he died a martyr and got a sainthood out of it. Beheading and braining someone in a church is rather horrific, don't you think? Mind you, killing someone in their bed isn't much better. Annie, do you mind bringing more coffee?" she called to the housekeeper, who was on the way out the door to the hall.

"I did some initial research on my laptop regarding your handyman," Rex told Phoebe in a low voice. "Couldn't find any criminal background on Alan Burke. Thought it worth checking even though you said he hasn't been to the house in a year."

"And I don't see what he would have had to gain by Dad's death."

Rex folded his napkin. "With no family besides yourself or many friends of your dad's here in Canterbury to look into, there's not much more I can do until I return to Edinburgh and speak to the clerk. His old chess partner might have been able to help us if he hadn't been mugged. And Christopher Penn had not seen your father at his shop in a while." He glanced over at his hostess. "Are you going to report the thefts to the police?"

Phoebe poured herself a mug of coffee from the thermal pot. "I'll do that. Maybe his album and watch will turn up in a pawnshop, as you suggested. Anything interesting in the paper?" she asked, indicating the refolded *Sunday Times* at his elbow. "Is that the photo of the missing girl?"

Rex passed the newspaper to her. "The police are pretty certain it's an abduction now. There's no boyfriend in the picture, and an old brown and beige Iveco van was spotted driving around the vicinity of the school on Thursday afternoon."

"Some pervert on the prowl, no doubt," Phoebe remarked in disgust, shaking out the paper. She looked across the table at Rex. "Are we still going on our outing?" she asked more brightly.

"Ready when you are. I checked the weather and we could not have asked for better for a leisurely stroll."

He kept Phoebe company while she finished her breakfast and afterwards he called his fiancée while his hostess went upstairs to find a pair of shoes suitable for their walk.

Located close to the city centre, Westgate Gardens comprised eleven acres of public park by the banks of the River Stour, providing a tranquil spot for families and couples both young and old. They had not gone far when the blue and orange flash of a kingfisher caught Rex's attention as it flitted over the colourful flowerbeds that bordered the narrow expanse of water.

"I used to bring Dad here when he first came to live with me," Phoebe said, taking Rex's arm and ambling beside him along the gravel path. "He was able to get about without the use of a cane then." She gave a heavy but not altogether unhappy sigh. "He so enjoyed the wildlife and the punts."

They stopped to watch the long, squared-off wooden vessels glide by with their single boatman standing astern, steering with a pole as passengers bundled in parkas and fleece jackets took in the views from the water. Phoebe decided she didn't want to go out on the river after all, which looked cold and uninviting even on this mild October morning, the breeze ruffling up ripples on the grey surface. Suddenly she shrieked and jumped backwards, eliciting surprised glances from passers-by on the path.

"Whatever is the matter?" Rex asked, following her fixed stare. He spotted a sleek rodent by the bank a second before it turned tail and disappeared among the plant stems. "It's a water vole," he said. "Quite harmless. It was more frightened of us, I think."

Phoebe tucked her arm back under his and touched her head to his shoulder. "Doug said my fear of mice and rats was a socially induced conditioned response, but that doesn't make my revulsion any the less. What about you? Do you have any phobias?"

"I do. Hippophobia. A fear of horses."

Phoebe laughed as she drew him back to the trail. "Really? Why?" she asked with a quizzical glance.

"They have big teeth and unpredictable hooves, and they don't like me. I got thrown from one when I was a lad, and, though I was not badly injured, I never felt the urge to get back on one."

"I fear death more and more," Phoebe confided gravely. "I lost my mum quite young, which was an awful shock, of course, but Dad's death has given me an even greater sense of my own mortality." She gave a deep sigh.

"He had a long life," Rex said in an attempt to console her. "And an illustrious legal career that not many can boast of."

"I haven't done much with my life," Phoebe lamented, staring at the path ahead of them. "Doug was the career-minded one, the brilliant psychologist. I simply made the travel arrangements and read drafts of his books, though much of it went over my head."

Rex squeezed her arm with his. "They say behind every great man is a great woman."

His companion smiled up at him. "Well, you do know how to cheer a person up, Rex," she said.

Then he had achieved at least one small thing this weekend, he reflected. "Hungry yet?" he asked.

"Famished. It's been a while since I had this much exercise and fresh air. It's nice to be able to walk here from the house. I should do it more often."

They found a local pub with a beer garden. The sun peeked out from behind the clouds, brightening the grass and warming the wooden bench at the trestle table.

Phoebe loosened her gold-threaded green scarf and pulled a pair of sunglasses from her bag. "Now tell me all about your fiancée," she said, turning towards him.

A girl came just then to take their order, a Guinness for Rex, a cider for Phoebe, and a Ploughman's Lunch for two.

"Well," he replied when they were alone again. "Her name's Helen and she works as a school counsellor in Derby."

"Younger than you?"

"By five years."

Phoebe sniffed. "Brunette, blonde?"

"Blonde."

"Where did you meet?"

"In Sussex, some years ago." Rex removed his jacket. "It was on my first private case. I was visiting an old school friend of my mother's for Christmas. She'd converted her manor house into a hotel, and Helen was staying there with her friend Julie."

"And when's the wedding?"

The inevitable question. "It keeps getting postponed. It was all but set for this year, but other events got in the way. Helen can't quite make the decision to pack in her job and leave all her friends and move to Edinburgh. She likes Edinburgh well enough, mind, but it would mean pulling up roots."

"I pulled up roots when I left Edinburgh to get married," Phoebe countered. "I don't see why she can't make the sacrifice. And you can't move to England. It would mean giving up your QC-ship and everything you've worked so hard for."

"Helen has worked hard too," he said, rushing to his fiancée's defence. "My mother, who's getting on, would expect us to live with her. It's a big house and she can't afford its upkeep on her own, and so I live there most of the time."

Helen, understandably, had reservations about such an arrangement. She was used to having her own place, and setting out on married life under a mother-in-law's roof at their age was hardly ideal. However, there did not seem to be a viable alternative.

Phoebe rubbed a finger over a knot of wood on the table. "I could be persuaded to move back to Edinburgh, much as Canterbury has become my home."

"Aye," was all Rex could come up with. Was Phoebe hinting that he should be looking at her as a more suitable match? It made him think he had not been wrong about her behaviour after dinner the previous night. He spotted the waitress bringing their tray of drinks across the grass, adroitly sidestepping a toddler who was evading his fraught mother and chortling with glee.

"Grand," Rex said, taking up his glass tankard of stout and sinking his lips into the foam, grateful that he had again been spared an awkward moment. He savoured the clean and bitter taste before letting the first gulp slide down his throat.

Phoebe sipped at her drink. Her sunglasses masked her eyes, but he felt she might be pondering her next move, which he would be forced to parry. Would she report the theft of her father's possessions to the police or had she brought him to Canterbury on false pretences? He had not found any tangible clues in the judge's alleged murder; perhaps because there were none to begin with.

NINE

WHEN REX LEFT ST. Dunstan's Terrace to return to Edinburgh, all the media was talking about, on Annie's television when he went downstairs to say goodbye and on Phoebe's car radio on the way to the station, was the disappearance of the schoolgirl from Dover, now missing for three full days. News racks displayed photos of the dimpled fourteen-year-old, and posters had begun to appear in shop windows.

His own case was progressing no faster, and, much as he'd had an interesting time in Canterbury, he was glad to return to his mother's house in Morningside where, as he had told Phoebe, he lived during the week and most weekends when not visiting Helen in Derby or staying at his country lodge in the Highlands.

Miss Bird, his mother's aging companion and erstwhile housekeeper, met him at the front door.

He had called his mother upon arriving at Waverley Station and tea was waiting for him in the parlour, complete with the Royal Doulton china and paper doilies. He kissed his mother's snowy head and sat down beside her.

"Now tell us all aboot your trip to Canterbury," she said as Miss Bird, a diminutive woman with beady eyes reminiscent of currants, joined them at table and poured the tea.

He described the sights, specifically the ancient castle ruins and the soaring spires and stained glass windows of the cathedral. He remembered the engraving he had tucked among the clothes in his bag and which he would fetch down after tea when he unpacked. He went on to tell his mother and Miss Bird about Christopher Penn at whose shop he had purchased the souvenir, and he detailed the case Phoebe Wells had asked him to take on, without expressing his growing doubts regarding her motives.

"Not much to go on," his mother concluded.

"Noo," Miss Bird agreed. "And why did she not call the police if she thought her father was murdered?"

Rex helped himself to an iced bun from the three-tier cake stand. "She said she would file a report for the missing items, but she doesn't feel she has enough evidence to bring up her suspicion of murder."

"But the more time that goes by, the more evidence might be lost," his mother pointed out in surprise.

"I agree, Moira," Miss Bird said. "Either she believes it or she doesna. What are ye going to do, Reginald?"

Miss Bird had been their housekeeper since he was a boy, and she and his mother persisted in calling him by his given name, instead of its derivative "Rex," which he preferred. Now that they were well into their eighties he had lost all hope of their changing the habit.

"Tomorrow I'm seeing someone who worked with Judge Murgatroyd," he informed them. "Beyond that, I don't know."

"I remember Phoebe Wells as rather a highly strung young woman," his mother commented as she poured him more tea. "I hope you've not embarked on a fool's errand, Reginald. But I understand why you feel you had to offer your assistance. Her father did favour you, after all."

She spoke in the genteel tones of Morningside ladies, which Rex often thought belied a razor sharp mind that had lost none of its acuity in her advancing age. Helen had remarked how his mother reminded her in appearance and depth of perception of Miss Marple, and Rex had laughed and been forced to agree. Fortunately, however, Moira Graves did not meddle in his cases, professional or private. She and Miss Bird simply liked to offer arm-length opinions and applaud him on his success when deserved.

Once again, he doubted whether success in this case was even an option, since there might be no case at all.

After tea, he went upstairs and rang Helen. One wall of his boyhood room had been knocked through to the next bedroom and the new space remodelled to accommodate a private bath and a small study-cum-lounge. His personal suite notwithstanding, his mother had designated a separate room in the draughty Victorian house for his fiancée when she came to stay.

He stood at the window, mobile phone in hand, gazing over the walled back garden where an ancient elm provided shade in summer. Blackbirds flocked to the grey stone birdbath on the lawn, which was now filled with rainwater. A wrought-iron feeder containing black sunflower seeds was attached to the outside of his window and attracted starlings and great tits, and on occasion a Spotted Woodpecker, which he liked to watch when he got ready for work in the morning. Helen answered promptly.

"Hello, lass, I'm back home. Did you have a good day?"

"I went jogging with Jill after we spoke this morning, and then met Julie for lunch. I was just watching the news about the girl who's gone missing in Kent, not far from where you were staying."

"Aye, Dover is about half an hour's drive from Canterbury."

"It's not looking good," Helen predicted. She counselled teenagers at her school and Rex understood this would be a subject close to her heart. "It doesn't matter how often you tell young girls not to walk home by themselves, they think they're immune from danger at that age. She was wearing her school uniform and carrying a satchel. You'd think someone would have noticed her crimson blazer with the school emblem if she'd run away. Unless she had packed some clothes and left them with a boyfriend her family knew nothing about..."

"It appears more likely she was abducted. There's even speculation she was taken to France and sold into the white slave trade."

"Smuggling is easier with the Chunnel, I suppose," Helen said despondently.

"Kent Police staffs a station in Coquelles on the French side to deal with border crimes," Rex reminded her, referring to the village near Calais where the Eurotunnel terminal was located. "Hopefully, if it's a case of abduction, the person or people involved won't get far."

"You seem well-informed," Helen said in a way that told Rex she was smiling.

"I had time to read the Sunday papers on the train since I've not made much headway in my own case." He relayed his suspicions regarding Phoebe's intentions towards him. "I think she may have made up or exaggerated the part concerning her father's murder. She's clearly lonely after losing both him and her husband, and in need of company."

"Be careful, Rex. I know what a big teddy bear you are, but she may mistake your kindness for something more and get her heart broken if her feelings are unrequited."

"Well, of course they're unrequited! I have no romantic interest in the woman."

"I'm just saying … Remember what happened with Moira."

Moira Wilcox, the girlfriend preceding Helen and who shared his mother's first name, had attempted suicide after he broke up with her. It had been a tragic and messy business, and had almost cost him his relationship with Helen.

"Did she make a pass at you?" she enquired.

Rex scratched his ear as he stared across the garden now disappearing into shadow, lying as it did on the east side of the tall house. "Ehm, I'm not sure. She got a wee bit tipsy last night … "

"And?"

"I think she may have hoped I might kiss her. But she apologized this morning. And she asked a lot aboot you."

"There, you see? She's jealous. Probably a good idea if you don't go back to Canterbury."

"I don't see that I'll have cause to. As of right now, there's no case. Can you come up to Edinburgh next weekend?"

"I'll try." Helen sounded reassured and sent a kissing sound over the phone as they bid each other a tender good night.

A long-distance relationship wasn't easy, but Rex was determined to make it work. Perhaps Helen could be persuaded to make a permanent move. Phoebe's words had unsettled him. He hoped Helen cared enough to make the sacrifice. And then he asked himself if he could turn his back on Edinburgh.

TEN

AT HIS CHAMBERS ON Monday, Rex conducted an informal interview with the former clerk of court, Andrew Doyle, an obliging and mannerly old gentleman with a precise Scottish enunciation, in spite of his quavering voice.

"I miss the old place," he said, his hands resting on the engraved silver knob of his walking cane. He looked about him at the fastidious décor, file folders neatly stacked on cabinets, books arranged in their proper order on the shelves, the desk itself devoid of clutter, while still bearing the accoutrements of an office not yet gone paper-free.

Two framed photographs sufficed to grace Rex's workspace, a portrait of Helen and a picture of his son Campbell in cap and gown, holding up his scrolled degree in marine science from Jacksonville University in Florida.

"Retirement is not what it's cracked up to be, you know," Doyle warbled, shaking his nubby skull mapped with blue veins. "Dog-walking and gardening, for the most part. But my wife's happy to have me at home. Gordon Murgatroyd would likely have stayed on the bench if Lords Commissioners of Justiciary didn't have to retire at seventy. He took his position very seriously, as he should. You said you wanted to pick my brains in his regard. Well, pick away, Mr. Graves. I have all the time in the world."

Rex first offered his guest tea, which Doyle accepted. "The truth of the matter is his daughter is not convinced he died of natural causes," he told his visitor, "although there's no hard evidence to prove otherwise; only a set of unusual circumstances. But I agreed to look into it, and, naturally, I'm relying on your discretion."

"Naturally." Doyle had sat attentively during Rex's explanation, sipping tea from his cup beneath a clipped white moustache. "Well, now," he said. "His Lordship had been living in Kent all these years with little contact with me or anyone else, as far as I know. Not sure how I can help."

"According to his daughter, he became something of a recluse," Rex agreed. "I lost touch with him myself, I regret to say, other than sending a card and brief news at Christmas. He maintained a regular correspondence with very few people. I can only conclude that his murder, if such it was, is linked to his old life here. I'm left considering contentious cases at court. Someone he sentenced who might have held a grudge."

"Contentious, not so much," Doyle answered deliberately. "Controversial, perhaps. The Pruitt case readily comes to mind. Do you remember that one?"

Rex's heart went still. The investigation came back once again to Richard Pruitt. "Indeed I do. He was connected to a murder almost on our doorstep."

"Skinner's Close. Sinister name, I always thought." Doyle nodded to himself. "Of course, many of those names hark back to back-alley occupations: Fleshmarket Close, Surgeon's Close, and what have you. Aye, Pruitt's story was flimsy to say the least, and he looked like someone people could conceive of stalking a schoolgirl. Still, the jury must have had their doubts to come back with a 'not guilty and don't do it again' verdict." The old man chuckled knowingly. "It was one of Lord Murgatroyd's last cases. Don't see Pruitt murdering the judge, though, do you? Where would be the motive?"

"Do you recall him sending the judge a stamp?"

Doyle nodded. "I do. I personally thought Pruitt owed him more than a postage stamp. His Lordship should rightly have thrown the book at him in the public's opinion, but he could admonish the witnesses, even expert witnesses, with a withering look and all but get the jury to return the verdict he wanted."

Rex recalled that look very well. An image of the red-and-white-robed judge huddled in his chair and glowering beneath his bench wig flashed upon him as though it were yesterday.

"How aboot cases where the verdict crushed the accused?" he quizzed Andrew Doyle.

"Well, now, what judge does not have his share of outraged inmates? I imagine many of them eat, drink, and dream revenge. Judges do get murdered, but you'd think in the case of an old man they'd just let nature take its course."

"As perhaps it did." Rex sighed. He was probably wasting his time. "Aye, well, if you do remember anyone who threatened him in any significant way, perhaps you could let me know."

"I shall." Doyle deposited his cup and saucer on the desk. He paused in thought and lifted a bony finger. "Off the cuff, you could look into Don MacDonald and Scott Priest. Lord Murgatroyd sent MacDonald down for life for stabbing his shrew of a wife. MacDonald raised his fist at him from the dock. Priest shot two security guards in that Princes Street bank robbery in the late eighties, not fatally, I might add, and got life as well. Hurled insults at His Lordship as he was led away. But he'll still be in prison, as well. So, unless either of them got a released cell mate or outside contact to go down to Canterbury to murder the judge … However, Dick Whitely, who planted that bomb at Parliament House; remember him? He'd be oot by now."

"I applaud your memory," Rex said, smiling at the old clerk and yet daunted by the task ahead of him. He would have to go through the judge's cases and see which felons had been released in the past year or so. It could prove to be not only a tedious but futile process of elimination. He thanked Doyle and suggested they meet for lunch the following week, when Rex had a less packed schedule.

Conducting a private case on top of his court ones could hardly have fallen at a worse time. However, he would not be satisfied until he had, to the best of his ability, fulfilled his promise to Phoebe and his personal obligation to her father. To achieve this end, he would have to take her request for his help at face value.

He would start with Richard Pruitt, who'd had as much contact with the judge as anyone outside his home in the latter years. It was quite possible Gordon Murgatroyd had confided in the man who owed him his freedom.

Rex discovered that Pruitt's number was ex-directory and he was obliged to ring Phoebe. She finally located the number in her father's address book and asked Rex if he was getting anywhere.

He told her about his meeting with Andrew Doyle, who had given him the names of men who had, in their view at least, received harsh sentences from her father and might have plotted and executed revenge, even if through a third party. He asked in return if she had filed a police report for the missing items, and she said that she had. He assured her he would be back in touch as soon as he had anything concrete.

When he called Richard Pruitt's number, he received a recorded message and left one of his own. An hour went by, and then two more as he worked on court briefs. Quite possibly, the once-accused child murderer wanted to be left alone, and just when Rex had convinced himself that this was the case, his mobile phone rang and he saw Pruitt's number on the display.

"Thank you for returning my call, Mr. Pruitt."

"When you said it was concerning Gordon Murgatroyd, I just had to ring you back. I was devastated to hear the news, though at his age it's hardly surprising, is it?" Pruitt had a reedy and not altogether pleasant voice.

"Indeed. I won't take up too much of your time. It concerns a stamp in his collection. His daughter said it was from you."

"What of it, Mr. Graves?" Pruitt asked amiably enough.

"Nothing in or of itself, probably. I'm looking into a personal matter for her."

Pruitt gave a sigh of resignation over the phone. "You said in your message you were a QC and were acquainted with Judge Murgatroyd. I expect you know I was on trial for the stabbing of a young girl."

"It's not my intention or business to retry you in my own mind," Rex assured him. "A jury already passed judgement."

"I found her face-down in the close and tried to render assistance," Pruitt volunteered nonetheless. "That's how her blood got on me. A passer-by dialled police, said he'd seen me dumping her body. That was a lie, and they never located that particular witness. I had an alibi. I'd been at a pub and was heading home. It wasn't my usual local, and it was dark in there. I paid cash and no one remembered me. Another witness said I was behaving suspiciously. I was just trying to cover the poor lass up. It was cold that night. I didn't realize at first she was dead. A jury of fifteen acquitted me."

"The verdict was 'not proven,'" Rex qualified.

"That is correct," Pruitt conceded over the phone. "But Judge Murgatroyd was presiding and he let it be known that he thought the case against me was spurious. When I found out he was a collector of stamps, I sent him one from the States with the scales of Justice on it as a mark of gratitude and of my esteem. He thanked me, even though the stamp wasn't anything much, and said it was a wonderful addition to his collection. We kept in touch by letter and I gave him tips, being a professional stamp dealer."

"Did anyone know you were in contact with him?" Rex asked.

"Not from me."

"Was the girl's killer ever caught? I don't recall any recurrences."

"April Showers was her name. Pretty name, I always thought, though rather poignant in the event: short-lived, like April showers… No, the real culprit was not caught, but I pursued my own line of inquiry to aid in my defence, and I continued after the trial in the hope of restoring my reputation. I had to close up shop, you know, and now I work mostly online where most people don't know of my past. To this day I live under a cloud of suspicion."

Rex thought the man sounded sincere, but criminals were often good at deluding others and sometimes themselves. "Did anything come up in your own investigations?"

"Shortly after my trial a man went to prison for housebreaking. A thirteen-year-old girl was living at the residence, but he said he went in solely to steal valuables. She found him in her room with a knife and pushed a panic button. Her father came to her rescue. She was unharmed, but had a narrow escape, if you ask me."

"*Stouthrief*," Rex said, giving the Scottish legal term for armed burglary. "What was the man's name?"

"Dan Sutter. He was recently released from Shotts Prison. I've kept tabs on him to see if he'd get up to his old tricks. I hired a private investigator. I think Judge Murgatroyd believed he was up to more than just stealing, and that's why he gave him ten years, when no charges could be brought against him for attempted assault on a minor."

"That's a bit unorthodox," Rex remarked; even by Gordon Murgatroyd's standards, he thought.

"He had his own way of meting oot justice," Pruitt opined. "It may have made him a lot of enemies, but I admired him for it. Not many people have the strength of their convictions the way he had."

"Mr. Pruitt," Rex said, glancing at his watch. "Can you meet me late this afternoon? I'd like to discuss with you further."

"With pleasure. Can you come to my home? I live at Ramsay Garden. I don't venture oot much."

"I can be there by six."

Pruitt gave him his flat number and told him he would show him what he had on Sutter. Rex was still pensively holding the silent phone to his chin when Alistair entered his office bearing two cups and saucers. His friend never drank tea from less than the best bone china.

"I saw your door was open and thought you might be in need." Alistair spoke with a more Etonian than Scottish accent, having been educated in England, although Rex fondly suspected it was something of an affectation. His friend was rarely serious, unless he was prosecuting, and even then he was prone to a brand of irony that often had the back of the courtroom in a joyous uproar, forcing the judge to restore order.

Alistair set the cups down on the desk, nudging aside the crockery from Rex's previous visit, and folded his long form into the vacated chair. "Wasn't that old Doyle I saw earlier on?"

"Aye. He kindly came in upon my request." Rex proceeded to fill Alistair in on developments in his private case.

"I met Phoebe Wells one time," his colleague mused aloud. "She's quite stylish, as I recall, but not really your sort."

"Helen is my sort."

"Well, I wish you'd just hurry up and marry the woman. You know how I love weddings."

Rex gazed at his friend in mild frustration. "Alistair, this is a serious matter I'm dealing with. I didn't ask for it, but there it is."

"I'd go with you to Pruitt's house, but I have a fencing match." Alistair cut a fine figure, not only in his fine Savile Row suits, but also in his white fencing attire, especially when he pulled off his meshed helmet to reveal his Byronic locks and precision-cut sideburns.

"I doubt Richard Pruitt will pose a threat." Rex recalled a slightly built, even effeminate, man at the time of his trial. "He swears blind he's innocent."

Alistair gave a derisive laugh. "Don't they all?"

ELEVEN

PERCHED ABOVE THE TREETOPS on a hill of black volcanic rock rising above Princes Street, Ramsay Garden boasted enviable views and a central location by Edinburgh Castle. Town planner Patrick Geddes, who as a botanist had discovered chlorophyll in plants, had expanded on the original Scots Baronial design in the late nineteenth century, and nowadays the landmark cluster of red-roofed town homes, replete with whimsical towers, balconies, and half-timbered white gables, could fetch upwards of half a million pounds sterling apiece.

Rex had not been back here since visiting an old friend and erstwhile professor at the university, whose oriel window in the main reception room had looked upon the esplanade of the castle. They had sat at the window on long summer nights enjoying the stirring sound of bagpipes from the Royal Edinburgh Military Tattoo as men in kilts and bearskins marched in unison beneath the flood lights. Rex concluded Pruitt must be a highly successful stamp dealer to be able to afford a flat on prestigious Castlehill in spite of the adversity that had befallen him, justifiably or otherwise.

He parked his Mini Cooper in the residents' courtyard and crossed to Pruitt's block, burrowing his hands in the pockets of his camel hair coat. The weather had turned chilly with the onset of evening.

Finding the number he was looking for, he rang the bell and was immediately buzzed through to an internal stone stairway leading to a small terrace and a front door. It opened before he could knock and Pruitt, in a blue pullover and jeans, greeted him with a shake of the hand.

"Find the place all right?" he asked, ushering Rex inside a flat full of nooks and alcoves.

"Aye. I had a friend who lived around the corner. Redecorating, I see," Rex commented upon noticing pictures missing from the wall in the hallway, which left behind hooks and ghostly shapes amid the framed glass cases of what Rex assumed were rare postage stamps, some of them crinkled and bearing smudged markings.

"Just switching some stuff around. You know how it is." Pruitt showed him into the sitting room where one entire wall exhibited anthropological artefacts of warlike aspect, deadly spears and painted masks among them, from remote parts of the world. The man was obviously an avid and diverse collector.

"Where are these from?" Rex asked. "My friend collected such pieces."

"Indonesia, New Guinea ... Wherever I can find them."

The remaining walls, of pale pearlescent grey crowned with crisp white moulding, gave the space a sophisticated and airy feel and offset the choice antiques to perfection. Rex could not but notice that his host looked out of place in it, his dress not as dapper as the décor, aside from the rings on his fingers, and he appeared to have put on weight since his arrest many years before.

Pruitt invited him to take the window seat, even though the shades were drawn over the view, and offered him whisky. Rex willingly accepted, saying a dram would warm him up nicely.

"Aye, winter will be upon us before we know it," Pruitt said cheerily as he left the room.

Rex removed his coat and tartan scarf and placed them beside him. Pruitt returned shortly with the drinks on a tray. The gemstones on his pinkies drew Rex's attention back to his fingers, thick and red as raw sausages. After serving him, Pruitt sat down on a striped silk Regency chair, separated from his guest by a midnight blue rug. The recessed lights in the ceiling were set low, the flat peacefully quiet and comfortably heated.

Rex took a generous sip of his single malt. "How is the stamp business these days?" he asked, commencing the topic of conversation he was here to pursue.

"Up and down," Pruitt said. "A lot of foreign buyers."

"I don't know if I mentioned it on the phone, but one of the judge's albums went missing from his daughter's house. Not the one with your stamp in it. A new collection he had begun."

Pruitt started in surprise at the mention of his stamp. "Oh, aye. Glad it's still there. And how is the legal business these days?" he countered.

"Up and down," Rex replied, and they both drank.

"Must be satisfying to help put criminals away," Pruitt said, "And then be able to go home to dinner."

"I can live with it so long as I'm convinced they're guilty. Which wasn't the case with you," Rex hastened to add. "You were going to fill me in on your suspect in the April Showers murder in Skinner's Close," he prompted.

"Found in Skinner's Close, not murdered there."

"Right. You said you found the body. I don't think the police ever discovered the actual scene of the crime, did they?"

"No."

They both drank some more. Rex began to wonder why Pruitt was more reticent about discussing his suspect in person than on the phone, when he had seemed so anxious to exonerate himself by pointing a finger at someone else.

Rex loosened his tie. "You said the case has had a negative impact on your stamp business. I'm glad to see you seem to be doing all right for yourself, nonetheless." He felt he was not expressing himself as precisely as usual, his thoughts fleeing and losing focus.

Pruitt raised his tumbler. "To Judge Murgatroyd. His equal will never be among us again," he added in Scots Gaelic.

"Aye, *slàinte!*" Rex toasted in turn and sipped more slowly of his whisky, soon realizing it was the drink that was making him drowsy, not simply the pleasant warmth of the room and a busy day in chambers. He perceived his host watching him from across the blue carpet.

"Aye, it's easy to be holier than thou when you're living in a nice part of town like Morningside and not in a slum," Pruitt was saying through an emerging fog.

Was he referring to him or to Judge Murgatroyd, who had also lived in Morningside, before he moved to Canterbury? "Did you grow up in a slum?" Rex asked. He had never had cause to probe into Richard Pruitt's background. April Showers' murder had not been his case.

"Aye, but I've come a long way since then," his host replied, a meaty hand sweeping the air and indicating the refined surroundings.

His voice sounded rougher than on the phone that afternoon, or perhaps Rex was imagining it. And yet he'd had a similar impression upon arriving at the flat, before dismissing it almost instantaneously.

After all, people often did sound different on the phone, projecting their voices or sounding more formal, especially in business situations.

"Indeed you have. Come along way." Rex began to get an uncomfortable feeling over and above the sleepy sensation that was sweeping over him. He pulled back his shoulders and stretched open his eyes in an attempt to wake himself up. "This is potent whisky," he remarked. "I'm literally seeing double!" There appeared to be two of Pruitt on the far side of the blue Oriental rug.

"It must indeed be potent to put a big man like yourself oot," Pruitt said with what Rex took to be a smirk. He couldn't be sure since the light on the other side of the shades was dim and the room not much brighter.

He felt he was losing control of his mental and physical faculties but made a concentrated effort to stand up. "I should be going," he blurted. "I think I might be coming down with something. I'll return another time to discuss the … You know." He had forgotten exactly what he was here to discuss.

"Och, sit yourself down. It'll pass. I'll make some coffee."

Rex had no option but to sink back into the window seat. He felt almost too sluggish to move, let alone drive. "Aye, thanks. Coffee would be grand."

Pruitt got up from his chair and left the room. Rex leant back against the padded bench rest. He wrestled his phone from the pocket of his trousers and called Alistair to see if he could get a lift home, expecting to go through to voicemail. His friend answered immediately.

"Something's amiss," Rex slurred into the phone, but that was as far as he got. Pruitt had returned to the room with a thick coil of rope in his hand. "I'm at … "

Rex tried speaking again, but he could not recall the house number, and before he could remember it, Pruitt swiped the mobile from his hand and sent it tumbling to the floor. Rex heard it crunch under his boot. He fought to keep his wits about him, but it was a losing battle.

And yet he knew he could not give up. He had seen that soulless look in a man's eyes before.

TWELVE

"Who are you?" Rex stumbled to his feet only to be pushed back down on the window seat by the man in the blue pullover.

Before he could react, his hands were brusquely bound behind his back, and when he struggled, his assailant pulled out a jagged knife from the front pocket of his jeans and snarled at him to be still. With his free hand he looped one end of the rope around Rex's neck and tightened the noose. Rex's head jerked back and he could no longer utter a word.

The man crouched on the carpet and proceeded to tie Rex's ankles together. At that moment, the buzzer sounded in the hall and he spun around towards the door and cocked an ear.

He glanced over his handiwork and, apparently satisfied, crept into the hall. Rex watched as best he could, but the rope kept him in a stranglehold.

"Who is it?" his kidnapper asked, out of his sight.

Rex could not hear the answer. The man asked if the visitor was alone. The buzzer went again. Did the man have an accomplice? Rex began to panic in earnest. Were they going to take him away and dump his body somewhere? The rope bit mercilessly into his neck, and he could not move his wrists or ankles. Even if he managed to get to his feet, he wouldn't be able to walk, let alone run. He heard the front door open and a familiar voice demand, "Where is he?"

"In there," the man answered as the door closed. "Why don't you join us?"

Rex heard a surprised cry, halfway between a groan and a shout, and then the sound of two men engaged in a fist fight. He remembered the knife in the man's possession and feared for his friend's life. He attempted to warn him, but no sound he managed to produce proved loud enough.

A series of punches ensued and one of the men slammed into a wall with a grunt. Rex awaited the outcome in silent anguish and agony as he forcibly struggled against the coarse rope, chaffing his neck and wrists. He heard the wrenching open of the front door, followed by the thud of footsteps retreating down the stone stairway. Alistair burst into the room and stopped short when he saw Rex.

"What happened to you, old fruit?"

Rex made an impatient sound in his throat and squirmed within the confines of the rigging.

"Hold still while I loosen this." Alistair inspected the rope. "You look like a trussed up Christmas turkey. How on earth did you get into this bind?"

Rex all but gagged when his neck was freed. He touched tentative fingers to his scorched neck.

"I should go after him," Alistair said before Rex could get a word out of his mouth. His colleague tore out of the room as Rex attempted to gather his dulled wits.

Alistair returned ten minutes later, gasping for breath, one hand supporting himself against the wall of primitive exhibits, dislodging a tomahawk. "No sign of Pruitt in any direction. He'll no doubt be back at some point. Why in God's name did he attack you?"

"It's not Pruitt. Can you help untie my feet? My fingers are still tingling," Rex all but wheezed, wiggling his numb extremities. "I have poor circulation."

Alistair knelt on the floor. "In that case, he probably wouldn't have risked parking too close, if he drove here," he said, bending his head to the task of freeing Rex's feet. "Anyway, I alerted the police. That rope left a nasty mark on your neck. He almost choked you!"

Rex sat doubled over, massaging his ankles. "How did you get here so fast?" he asked through a dry mouth. "Not that I'm not thrilled to see you, of course." He would have hugged his friend, if only he could have stood up on his own.

"The fencing match was cancelled. My opponent has the flu. I was in the car when you rang. I tried phoning you back, but ... " He trailed off, seeing Rex's smashed mobile on the floor. "Luckily I found the bit of paper you wrote the address on discarded in the courtyard. Tsk-tsk, Rex. Littering!" Alistair stood over him, grinning like a fool.

"It must have fallen from my pocket," Rex protested feebly.

"You don't look well, old chum. And you sound drunk."

"He put something in my whisky. I feel disorientated. It's not the alcohol, I assure you. Only the rope cutting into my flesh helped prevent me from falling asleep."

Alistair pulled Rex up from the window seat and prodded his unsteady friend into the bathroom.

"The wallpaper's moving," Rex said in wonder. "I've never seen wallpaper do that before."

"It's not a novelty," Alistair told him. "He must have slipped you a hallucinogenic. My guess would be some sort of prescription sleep aid."

He forced Rex to throw up in the WC, after which Rex splashed his face with cold water from the basin. He looked at Alistair in the brightly lit mirror. "You don't look much better yourself. I heard you fighting in the hall."

Alistair regarded his handsome face, where a large red mark was blossoming over the left cheekbone.

"You should put some ice on that," Rex advised. "You can't go into court looking like you've been in a brawl. My collar and falls will cover my rope burn."

"The bruise is nothing." Alistair opened the panels of his coat. "That bastard lunged at me with a knife. Fortunately I was wearing my fencing jacket underneath, and the knife barely penetrated. At most I'll have a scratch."

"You're a lucky devil, Alistair Frazer."

"So are you. What would have happened if I hadn't been driving by Ramsay Garden?"

"I dread to think. I hope the police hurry up so we can leave."

His friend propelled him into the kitchen and plied him with glass upon glass of water from the tap. Rex drank thirstily, much as it hurt when he swallowed.

"He took care to rinse his glass." Alistair indicated the whisky tumbler on the draining board. "What about yours, I wonder?"

"He served it to me on a tray. My glass won't have his prints on it if he used a tea towel when filling it."

"If that wasn't Pruitt, I wonder who he is and where Pruitt is."

"Search me," Rex said, woozy still and reaching for a chair to hold on to for balance.

"The butcher's block here is intact. He may have brought the knife with him. Sit tight while I take a look around."

Rex did just that, his head flopping into his hands. He heard Alistair call out to him a few minutes later. Rex struggled to his feet and staggered towards his friend's voice, which had come from a room down the hall. "What is it?"

"I found Pruitt." Alistair was leaning into the fitted closet of a spare bedroom where none of the walls were the same size and the ceiling sloped steeply towards the window. Rex could not be sure whether this was by architectural design or if he was still reeling from the effects of his spiked drink, but at least the flowered Laura Ashley wallpaper was not moving.

"His hands are bound behind his back," he heard Alistair say. "His throat's been punctured. You'd better not look in your state. I think his attacker must have forced him in here before killing him. I didn't find blood anywhere else in the flat."

Rex's knees buckled beneath him and he keeled onto the double bed, whose floral duvet matched the walls.

Some time later, he felt someone shaking him. "Wake up, Rex. Wake up! He's alive. I need your help. Can you get up?"

Rex groaned and nodded groggily. "I was in a nightmare where I was being suffocated by giant flowers."

Alistair pulled him to his feet and together they lifted the injured man out of the closet, where he had lain with his chin on his chest, and moved him onto the bed.

"I called for an ambulance," Alistair murmured while examining the man's injured neck above the blood-drenched bow tie, which he removed. "Can you fetch some clean towels from the bathroom?"

On unsteady feet, Rex did as instructed. Alistair administered what emergency aid he could and assigned Rex the task of summoning the police again. Rex fumbled with Alistair's phone, pressing triple nine into it with exaggerated precision, and tried to deliver a coherent message.

The man lay motionless on the bed, his face ashen and his eyes closed, his breathing low and laboured. Alistair had wrapped a towel around his neck. He was asking for information about the assailant, but his patient remained unresponsive.

"His pulse is very weak," Alistair said. "John would know what to do, but he's not answering. He must be out on a call." He gazed over the prostrate man. "He is Richard Pruitt. I found his driving licence. I wish he could speak."

Rex was not surprised to have his identity confirmed. He more resembled the man he remembered from the news coverage ten years ago than the nondescript intruder who had served him the whisky. "He may be in shock, or else his throat might be damaged," he told Alistair. "I'm not sure there's much more you can do."

"How about you? You seem a little more lucid."

"It's an effort to keep my eyes open, but the fog's beginning to lift."

The police and ambulance arrived soon after at the same time. Rex and Alistair gave their statements and waited in the hall while the paramedics strapped Pruitt to a gurney in preparation for the descent down the steps to the car park.

Alistair pointed to the walls. "There are spaces where photos of the real Pruitt presumably were, which the pretend Pruitt didn't want you to see. Didn't that alert you to something being wrong?"

"Why would it? I didn't know they might be photos of Pruitt. I thought he was redecorating. You're always moving stuff around in your house. You're a right Martha Stewart."

"Touché."

When the detective, a harried and abrupt chief inspector by the name of Pete Lauper, was finished with his questions, the two men left the flat and Alistair drove Rex home. He assured him he and John, his live-in partner, would pick up the Mini Cooper later.

So as not to alarm his mother, who sometimes waited up for him past her bedtime, Rex had draped his scarf around his bruised neck. He found her reading in the parlour, wrapped in a wool dressing gown. Bending to kiss her good night, he said he had been to dinner with his friend and would retire to his room directly, since it had been a long day.

Once upstairs, he made his nightly call to Helen, telling her the stamp dealer he had gone to see that evening was, for whatever reason, a marked man and was now being treated in hospital for a stab wound to the neck, dangerously close to the carotid artery.

"I just happened to wander into the aftermath," he explained. "The intruder bolted when Alistair arrived," which was not the whole story, but would have to suffice for now.

He had to tell her about the sedative in his drink, since he still sounded drunk, but postponed mentioning his being tied up and threatened with a knife. It would take too long and he would have to reassure her, and he didn't feel he could last much longer.

He sat on his bed and undid his shoe laces with one hand, his other occupied by the phone. Lacking proper coordination, the manoeuver proved all the more difficult.

"But you're okay?" Helen asked with concern.

"Grand. I just feel like I could sleep for a week."

"You should go to the hospital and get yourself checked out, maybe have your stomach pumped," she was saying. "Who knows what he put in your drink. And what if he's caught and you want to press charges?"

"I don't feel ill. I think it was only a strong sleeping pill crushed up in my whisky. Anyway, I can't think of that now, lass." He yawned and Helen reluctantly said she would let him go, but she made him promise to call her as soon as he woke up the next morning.

He got as far as removing his suit jacket before collapsing on the bed. Just as sleep came to claim him a memory surfaced, which he felt might be important. He must remember to ask Alistair, he thought frantically before finally succumbing to utter oblivion.

THIRTEEN

THE FOLLOWING MORNING REX sat down to breakfast bright and early, feeling clear-headed and well rested after a deep, dreamless sleep. Fortunately, his mother wasn't down from her room yet. She was sure to make a fuss if she saw the rope burn, and he had already had a talking-to from Helen that morning on the phone about the danger he subjected himself to in his private cases. He had finally described to her the extent of his injuries and how the man had produced a knife, which he had tried, with limited success, to use on Alistair.

He heard Miss Bird approach in the hall and adjusted his white wing collar and long neckties. He was due in court at ten, and so his garb was not out of place. He also had on the tail coat he would wear under his gown.

"Is something wrong wi' yer neck?" Miss Bird asked, entering with his breakfast and seeing him smooth down his falls.

"A bit of a sore throat," he said truthfully enough.

"I'll fetch ye some lozenges," she said. "And I'll make chicken broth for yer dinner." In her mind, he was still Wee Reginald in school shorts and cap.

"Sit down and have a cup of tea, Miss Bird," he urged, not that she ever ate breakfast with them.

"Och, I had my tea and porridge a while ago, and I need to get on."

She left the parlour and Rex tucked into his cooked breakfast, washing it down with great quantities of tea. He felt unaccountably cheerful and famished, in spite of, or due to, the excitement last night. He put it down to adrenalin and a lucky escape.

The street outside was stirring to life. Through the net-curtained window he could hear people on the pavement walking their dogs, taking their children to school, and getting an early start on their grocery shopping at Waitrose. Buses rumbled along their route on a nearby road while the frequency of cars passing by the house increased with the advancing hour.

He folded his newspaper. It had now been five days since the schoolgirl in Kent had gone missing, and there were no new developments, at least none that were made available to the public. The brown and beige van had not been found and no new witnesses had come forward. Rex could barely bring himself to imagine Lindsay Poulson's fate. Her father was a music teacher, and so it was unlikely she was being held for ransom. In any case, a demand would have been made by now.

Rex surmised that if she had been abducted and were still alive, the poor girl was probably wishing herself dead.

"Better take yer brolly," Miss Bird advised as he put on his overcoat in the hallway.

He did so when he spied the overcast sky outside the front door.

Upon arriving at chambers he saw that Alistair's door was ajar and found his friend standing at his desk sorting through a pile of documents.

"How are you, old fruit?" he asked upon seeing Rex.

"Wonderful. And you look a lot better."

"John saw to my shiner and managed to counteract the red with some green camouflage makeup. I just have to remember not to touch my cheek."

Rex asked if he still had the piece of paper that he had picked up off the ground with Pruitt's address on it. He had remembered it as he fell asleep the previous night and had recalled its importance again upon waking.

Alistair paused with a stapled sheaf of paper in his hand and shook his head. "I emptied my pockets when I got home, as I customarily do, and tossed it into the fireplace."

"Is it still there?"

"No, went up in smoke, my dear fellow. Was it important?"

"There was a name written on that bit of paper. Do you recall what it was?"

"I don't. Sorry. There were a few things scribbled down. I didn't think it was important."

"The name was Pruitt's suspect in the April Showers case. I called the hospital first thing this morning. He's oot of intensive, though not well enough to receive visitors."

"Let's hope he makes a full recovery."

"Aye, and I hope he can shed some light on what happened at his flat. He almost died. And you and I could have been killed too."

"Wrong place, wrong time," Alistair remarked. "But doesn't it make you feel more alive? I feel electrified! And there I was thinking this was going to be a humdrum sort of week."

"Humdrum sounds just fine with me. Not sure I could stand any more excitement. It was a close call, and I never even got the information I went there for in the first place. Right, well I best get going."

The two men arranged to get together for lunch at their favourite pub close by in the Lawnmarket.

Alistair dipped his head at Rex's court attire as he made to leave. "What's the trial again?"

"Man charged with murdering his stepson. Open and shut. He was caught on the nanny-cam around the time of the child's death."

"Can't get away with much nowadays, can you?" Alistair commented, busily bent over his papers with his hands planted on the desk.

Rex would bet Ramsay Garden was equipped with security cameras. He wished one had been installed at the back of Phoebe's house, and then he'd have proof that something nefarious had occurred. His thoughts turned briefly to her garden and its hexagonal whitewood summerhouse. She had left a message for him the previous evening, but he had not had a chance to return her call due to all the drama at Ramsay Garden.

When he reached his office, he closed his door and rang Phoebe to give her an update on Richard Pruitt. She was shocked to hear what had happened to her father's penfriend, but relieved that he had survived his ordeal.

"Does this have anything to do with Dad's murder?" she asked.

"Not necessarily." Rex flipped back the page of his desk calendar, checking his schedule. "Ramsay Garden could have been a house break-in gone wrong. I won't know more until I can speak to him. He's at the Royal Infirmary. They won't let anyone visit yet."

"I'm sorry I got you involved in all this. Are you all right?"

Rex told her only that he had been drugged, so as not to alarm her, and added, "When I met whom I thought to be Pruitt at his home, he was not wearing the bow tie I remember from the media coverage a decade ago. And he sounded different than on the phone, though he didn't say much in person, at least to begin with. He seemed different in a lot of ways, but I just assumed it was Pruitt."

"And people do change, especially when they've been through a lot," Phoebe said.

"In addition," Rex went on, "his impersonator didn't seem to know about the American stamp. That's when my antenna went up, but I was already under the influence of whatever he had put in my whisky. And then he attacked my colleague with a knife." Phoebe gasped at the other end of the line. "Fortunately Alistair was wearing his fencing jacket under his coat. The tournament he was supposed to have been competing in was cancelled, and he came to Ramsay Garden to assist me."

"I bet you, though, Pruitt is guilty of April Showers' murder," Phoebe said. "I always thought so in spite of what Dad might have thought. Why else would someone come after him if not seeking revenge? Have you looked into her family?"

"It's been over ten years," Rex said dubiously.

"Someone biding their time," Phoebe suggested. "Perhaps a relative. What if her mum died recently and April's dad decided to seek justice at last? Perhaps his wife dissuaded him from doing anything while she was alive."

"Or else Pruitt made an enemy in his stamp business or other activities," Rex said. "Did you know he collects third world weaponry and masks as well?"

"I always thought he was a bit strange when I saw him on TV. And I'm a little suspicious of aging bachelors. You always wonder if they have something to hide."

"My friend Alistair has never been married," Rex answered in amusement. "But I'm sure you'd find him quite charming. And very upfront."

"I'd like to meet him," Phoebe enthused. "Perhaps you could bring him on your next visit. I'd like to thank him for coming to your rescue. I wonder what your attacker planned on doing with you once you were knocked out by whatever he put in your drink?"

Rex refrained again from telling her about being bound at knife-point. He did mention, however, that Alistair had a live-in partner, which seemed to deflate her. He realized then that he had inadvertently raised her hopes. Simultaneously, his desk phone buzzed and someone knocked at the door. The work day was beginning in earnest. He assured Phoebe he would call again when he'd had a chance to visit Richard Pruitt in hospital.

"Be careful," she said with feeling. "I couldn't bear it if something happened to you."

FOURTEEN

DEACON BRODIE'S TAVERN ON the Royal Mile, in the Old Town, sported large arched windows and elegant black trim, but more importantly served craft ales to suit Alistair and good bar food to satisfy Rex. They went inside and found unoccupied seats at one of the tall tables arranged on the polished wood floor.

Rex ordered a Guinness and the haddock in batter with chips. He received a few curious glances, dressed as he was in his old-fashioned court clothes, and wondered if the customers took him for an historic tour guide or else a small-time actor on his lunch break. A Japanese tourist snapped a picture of him with his phone. Alistair raised a disapproving eyebrow at the man and another when Rex's plate arrived.

"Stodgy, much?" he asked.

"I missed dinner last night. Things got a little hairy at Ramsay Garden, if you recall."

Alistair fastidiously picked at his cheese and chutney sandwich and salad. "I haven't heard back from the detective. Have you?"

Rex shook his head. "Presumably the police have no leads yet. After all, we weren't able to give a really good description of the man, except for his clothes. He might have been wearing a jacket or something over his blue sweater when he attacked Pruitt because I didn't notice any blood on him. Other than that, he didn't really have any distinguishing characteristics to speak of."

"Just your average middle-aged bloke, pasty-faced and with a bit of a beer belly," Alistair agreed. "And thinning, sandy hair."

"I should have remembered Richard Pruitt had no hair." Rex scooped up a forkful of mushy peas. "Not even sure I could recognize him again at a distance. Pruitt might know who he is."

"Incidentally, John is friendly with a nurse on his wing. She'll be on duty this afternoon and can probably get you in for a visit if you say you're his brother or another family member."

"Not sure I want to be related."

"All in a good cause."

"I have to be back in court at two," Rex said. "But I'll drive over later, if I can."

"What I wouldn't give to catch that maniac," Alistair said between clenched teeth. "I'm sure he left Pruitt for dead. I'm equally sure you would have suffered the same fate."

"I hope he hasn't heard he likely failed in his attempt on Pruitt. While Pruitt's in hospital, he's safe enough. It's when he comes oot that worries me. We don't want our man coming back to finish the job."

"And us," Alistair said. "We're witnesses, after all. Better keep our eyes peeled until he's apprehended."

"If he's ever apprehended," Rex corrected. "It's all right for you. You're trained in the martial arts. I'm aboot as lethal as one of these chips." He pronged a limp strip of potato on his fork, almost wishing Phoebe Wells had never invited him to Canterbury and set him on this dangerous path.

FIFTEEN

MEDICAL PERSONNEL IN SCRUBS strode along the corridors in squeaky-soled shoes. A pair of nurses stood gossiping and giggling in a corner, but the overall atmosphere was grim. After all, there was no pleasant reason to be in hospital unless you were in the maternity ward, Rex reflected, and this was Men's Surgical. A patient swung past on a pair of crutches, one leg heavily bandaged to the knee.

Rex's escort led him into a small room smelling of antiseptic and consisting of six narrow beds on wheels, half of them empty, while two were occupied by seemingly comatose bodies. Rex unbuttoned his coat.

"Five minutes," the nurse told him in no uncertain terms, stopping at the foot of the last bed. "Talking is painful in his condition. Don't get him excited."

"Well, you look a sight better than when I last saw you," Rex announced upon seeing a more recognizable Pruitt, who was propped up against two hospital pillows, a large plaster stuck to his neck and secured by a bandage. The nurse left.

"No tubes, as you can see," Richard Pruitt rasped with obvious effort, offering a wan smile. "Breathing on my own now." Though weak, he seemed surprisingly cheerful. Rex thought perhaps he deemed himself fortunate to be alive, as well he ought, considering the nature of his wound. "What happened to your own neck?" the patient asked.

Rex rearranged his scarf to cover up his bruises. "Your impersonator nearly strangled me with a rope." He pulled a visitor's chair up to the bed.

"Oh." Pruitt winced. "I'm so sorry. I had no idea. I vaguely remember someone coming to my assistance."

"Alistair Frazer, a friend and colleague of mine."

"Well, it's mostly his voice I remember." He gazed myopically at Rex. An indentation on the bridge of his nose attested to the long use of eyeglasses. "What happened?"

Rex explained his side of events and asked Pruitt for his.

Pruitt looked at him sideways while he spoke, keeping his head immobile on the pillow. "He said on the phone he was interested in one of the early Victorian stamps I had listed. He wanted to see it in person since it was a bit pricey. I didn't think twice as buyers do sometimes come to my home."

He reached to the bedside table for his beaker of water and took a careful sip. "When he arrived, I simply buzzed him in. Stupidly, I never thought if I could find him, he could find me. But now you believe me, don't you, Mr. Graves?" Pruitt asked feverishly, straining his voice. Reflexively, his hand flew to the white bandage covering his throat and he sank back into the pillows.

"Don't exert yourself," Rex soothed, though eager to learn more. He waited until Pruitt had recovered sufficiently. "Who are we talking aboot?" he asked when the man's moon face had smoothed out again and he was breathing more evenly.

"Dan Sutter! I'll have to replace that incompetent private detective. Sutter must have spotted him when he was being tailed."

"Sutter," Rex repeated. That was the name he had jotted on the piece of paper that had fallen out of his pocket. "The man you think was responsible for assaulting April Showers and for whose murder you said you almost took the blame?"

Pruitt nodded and immediately groaned. "Must remember not to do that," he said with an attempt at a grin. "Judge Murgatroyd put Sutter away shortly after for burgling a home where a young girl resided. She sounded the alarm when she found him in her room."

"Aye, I remember you telling me that on the phone."

"I'm convinced he went in to molest her, but it couldn't be proved. He copped only to breaking into the house with intent to steal."

Rex got the distinct impression from the way Pruitt spoke that he watched American cop shows. "Where does Sutter live now that he's oot of prison?"

"In a hostel near Waverley Station." Pruitt took another sip of water and swallowed with difficulty.

"And you think he came to your home under the pretext of buying a stamp in order to kill you?"

"Because I know the truth regarding April Showers." Pruitt's voice came out in forced breaths. Sweat beaded his brow and bald, egg-shaped crown. "He murdered that girl and it's been my mission these past ten years to prove it and exonerate myself." He began to cough and splutter.

The nurse bounced back in the room and frowned at Rex. "It's been five minutes," she said, tapping the watch pinned to her tunic, before he could ask Pruitt what proof he had.

However, he didn't want to abuse the privilege she had accorded him in letting him visit the patient, which she had only done as a favour to Alistair's partner. Rex rose and told Richard Pruitt he would return when he felt stronger, and he asked what he could bring.

"Not grapes," the injured man rasped. "I can't eat solids yet. Books. Scottish history, if you would be so kind. You do believe me, don't you?" he insisted, turning his head and creasing his bandage in the process.

The nurse chided him for moving about and not taking care of his stitches.

"And chocolates for you," Rex said following her out of the hospital room.

Night had fallen by the time he left the building. He regained his car in the parking lot, and, just as he turned the key in the ignition, his phone vibrated in his coat pocket. He saw the call was from Phoebe Wells.

"Very timely," he said. "I've just left the hospital. Pruitt is on the road to recovery, I'm pleased to report."

"That's good," Phoebe said excitedly. "But what I was ringing about is that Annie unwittingly found a vital clue in my father's murder. I need you to come to Canterbury as soon as possible. It's really, really important!"

SIXTEEN

After Rex had spoken to Phoebe he rang Pete Lauper, the detective chief inspector he and Alistair had spoken to the previous evening at Ramsay Garden. He told him Pruitt's assailant was one Dan Sutter.

"And how do you know that?" DCI Lauper demanded. "You had no idea who the man was yesterday."

"I've just come from the hospital."

"You spoke with Richard Pruitt?" The detective sounded put out in the extreme. An irascible man with a permanent scowl, Rex had no difficulty picturing him at this moment. "And how did you manage that?"

"I, ehm, a nurse let me in for five minutes."

"Mr. Graves, you should have let me question him first. I understand you have an interest in solving murders in your free time, but this is my job. I was told Richard Pruitt was in no condition to receive visitors."

"He's still very weak. I was only permitted a visit as a special favour. I don't want to get the nurse in any trouble."

"Well, where is this Dan Sutter now?" the detective further demanded while Rex looked about him at the cars parked in long rows under the lights. "We only got an indistinct glimpse on the CCTV video camera of the man entering and leaving the Ramsay Garden tower," he griped.

"He lives in a hostel near the railway station."

"What else do you know about him?"

"He has a prior conviction for breaking into a house with a knife and served ten years at HMP Shotts. That's as much as I know." For now, Rex added to himself, his intention being to find out more.

"Well, thank you for that information," Lauper said with a heavy dose of sarcasm. "But I will conduct the search from now on, is that understood?"

"Understood." Rex bid him a civil goodbye and drove back to Morningside, mulling over his phone conversation with the apoplectic detective and also with Phoebe.

She had refused to tell him what the clue was in her father's murder, saying he would just have to "wait and see," as though it were some kind of game she was organizing for his amusement. He sighed. Now he would have to tell his fiancée that her trip to Edinburgh this weekend was postponed.

After dinner he went up to his rooms and worked through the files he had procured that day on the felons whom Judge Murgatroyd had convicted, making a list of possible suspects in his alleged murder. He excluded lifers and those too old to have accomplished the climbing feat required to get into Phoebe's house. For now he worked on the assumption that, if this was a crime of revenge, the perpetrator most likely would have wanted to exact the revenge himself.

The list turned out to be predictably long, comprising the worst of criminals, along with the Parliament House bomber, who had been released in time to murder the judge.

The whereabouts of each and every one would have to be looked into, unless Phoebe's latest clue panned out, a task he would relegate to his young friend Thaddeus. The well-connected techno whizz had assisted him in several private cases in return for Rex's influence in helping him secure a position at a prestigious law firm in London.

Rex next scoured the Web for any details he could find about the Showers family and was chagrined to find that April had been an only child. How her parents must have mourned her, especially as her body had been unceremoniously discarded in a back alley and the man charged with her murder had gone free. Mr. and Mrs. Showers would have had even more motive to do Pruitt harm than Dan Sutter had, Rex mused.

Presumably, Sutter had not appreciated the fact that Pruitt had put a detective on his tail and he had to keep looking over his shoulder after ten years spent inside a maximum security prison.

Rex sat back in his chair, cradling the back of his head in his hands. Perhaps he should leave the Pruitt/Sutter case to DCI Lauper, after all, and concentrate on the Murgatroyd investigation. The only reason he had contacted Pruitt in the first place was for information on the stamp he had given the judge, a stamp of no apparent value or significance. Certainly, Christopher Penn had not honed in on it when appraising the album. He hoped Phoebe had a more promising lead.

SEVENTEEN

THE NEXT MORNING REX told Alistair about his visit with Pruitt in hospital and how the detective had been cross with him for getting in to see him first.

Alistair laughed from behind his desk, where he sat in a posture of elegant repose, the bruise on his cheek much improved, or at least skilfully disguised.

"I got the impression DCI Lauper is always cross about something," he remarked. "Well, I'm glad you got the name you were looking for. I've been feeling perfectly awful for letting it go up in smoke, but, after all, you did drop it, and so I consoled myself that you could not justifiably condemn me for my own carelessness."

"If this is how you make your arguments in court, I'm surprised you're still practising law," Rex joked.

"Quite successfully, I should add," Alistair riposted. "Though I don't quite have your stellar record of convictions. How's the stepson case coming along?"

"Closing speeches tomorrow. If the jury can return a quick verdict, it's off to Canterbury for me at the end of the week."

"I thought you and Helen were going to join me for a round of golf."

"Phoebe Wells has more information regarding her father's murder."

Alistair arched a groomed eyebrow. "Somehow I feel sceptical."

"You look sceptical."

"Look, old chum. You went to see her last weekend, did a bit of digging, and came up short. I know you feel beholden to Judge M because the old ogre mentored you, but I'd say you have adequately fulfilled your self-imposed duty."

Rex scratched his ear. "Aye, but 'adequately' is not enough, and I can't be certain there's nothing in what Phoebe said."

"Phoebe Wells almost got you killed, however innocently. It might be prudent to give Pruitt a wide berth from now on. He has the police to protect him, and DCI Lauper appears to have made it quite clear he doesn't want your help."

"Well, he can pursue Sutter, and the best of luck to him. I'll be in Kent."

Alistair shrugged. "Don't get sucked in too deep. Helen might start getting the wrong idea."

"Helen has more sense. And, fortunately for me, she's very supportive of my 'morbid hobby,' as she calls it. I'll try to see her in Derby."

"Weren't you planning a wedding?" Alistair asked with a kind but pointed look.

"Aye," Rex said vaguely as he beat a hasty retreat from his friend's office. He was beginning to feel pressure from all sides. Even his mother had had something to say that morning about Helen's cancelled stay at the house. The sooner he got to the bottom of the Murgatroyd case, the better for everyone.

In the meantime, he was busy in court with his murder trial until the end of the week, when the jury took less than three hours to return a verdict of guilty on the Friday morning. Alistair rang to congratulate him. It was their custom to celebrate their wins with a drink at Deacon Brodie's Tavern, but Rex had to catch a train that afternoon to London and then on to Canterbury.

"I'll take a rain check," Rex said after apologizing profusely.

"And I'll take one for golf," his friend remarked. "What are friends coming to that you can no longer rely on them for golf or ale?"

"Come with me. Phoebe invited you as well."

"John and I have plans for the theatre tomorrow night. But please send Mrs. Wells my best."

Rex had packed his bag the night before, banking on the jury, who had been attentive during the trial and visibly receptive to his pleas for justice. He had learned to read jurors' reactions over the years, however much they strove to look neutral. It was in the blinks and stares, the set of their mouths, and body language. When he had them in his sway, they leaned forward and nodded, and even smiled. In this case, the accused's counsel had not been a worthy opponent, but, to be fair, she had not had much to work with. The cam-recording evidence had been especially damning.

Just as he was preparing to leave his office for the weekend, he received a phone call from DCI Lauper, who informed him, in a more conciliatory tone than he had used during their last conversation, that the police had searched Dan Sutter's room at the hostel. They had found no sign of him or the knife used against Mr. Pruitt, nor any of the fugitive's possessions. Sutter had done a flit.

"Can't have had much as he's been on the dole since his release from prison," Lauper said. "But information we found indicates he might have fled to the Outer Hebrides." The detective expelled a hiss of breath. "If he can get his hands on a boat, he could hide on any number of the islands up there. We've organized a manhunt. With any luck, we'll flush him oot of his hole."

The long chain of islands and skerries west of the northern mainland of Scotland was an isolated and remote area, ideal for hiding out if you could withstand the cold around this time of year and get hold of provisions. Rex did not envy the police their chances. A desperate man like Sutter would take no risk of getting caught and thrown back in the slammer, this time for life.

"I thought you'd want to know he's likely left the immediate vicinity, so you and your colleague can rest easy," Lauper added.

"I appreciate it, detective. Were you able to speak to Richard Pruitt?"

"I was. He's making a reasonable recovery, according to his doctor, but he won't be discharged much before the middle of next week."

Rex had planned to revisit Pruitt at the hospital, but work had intervened. He would go on Monday or Tuesday with the history books he had promised. He and the detective exchanged wishes for a pleasant weekend, and Rex rushed to the station with only minutes to spare.

Now that his work week was over, he could concentrate on his private investigation. Hopefully, the new clue that Phoebe's housekeeper had discovered would validate his time and effort on the Murgatroyd case.

EIGHTEEN

FOR THE SECOND TIME, Rex walked from Canterbury West Station to St. Dunstan's Terrace. Phoebe met him at the door. He had rung from London to let her know when his train was due in, but had insisted she not trouble herself to collect him unless it was raining. She wore a floral jersey dress and her hair was swept up in a tortoiseshell comb, which had the effect of lifting and rejuvenating her features.

"I hope you're starving," she declared. "Annie made more of her scones, since you liked them so much last time." She took his coat and led him through to the drawing room.

When Annie served the tea, Rex told her, "I'm dying to know what it is you found."

The housekeeper turned to Phoebe, who nodded for her to go ahead. "Well," she replied. "It was one of them clasps women wear in their hair."

"A hair-slide," Phoebe added. "Let me show you." She rose from the sofa and retrieved a small, long object from an antique writing desk by the window and handed it to Rex.

The metal clip was covered with pink and white chequered plastic. "So it is," he said.

"It doesn't belong to either of us," Phoebe told him.

Rex could not see such an item adorning Annie's grey wisps, nor could he imagine Phoebe putting something so cheap and frivolous in her lustrous dark locks. "Where did you find it?" he asked the housekeeper, who stood by the sofa with her hands folded against her apron.

"In the judge's mattress. I went to turn it before putting on the new bedding. It was tucked in one of them dimples around the buttons. And being as the mattress has pink roses on it, I never noticed it sooner. I took it straight to Mrs. Wells."

"How did it get in the mattress?" Rex wondered aloud.

"It must've fallen in there when I stripped the bed after Mr. Murgatroyd passed away."

"We were thinking it might have slipped from someone's hair," Phoebe said. "Most likely a girl's or young woman's. The mattress is less than two years old. I got it for Dad's bad back and bought it new. No one except Annie and I have been in his room since it was delivered all wrapped in plastic, so the hair-slide has to belong to someone who had no business being in his room."

"I see," Rex said, turning the metal part of the clasp between his fingers. "Pity there's no hair attached." He set it down carefully on the glass-top coffee table in the vain hope it might retain prints other than those of the two women known to have handled it. "And it looks like something mass-produced in China. Ten-a-penny, and therefore hard to trace."

"We don't see a man wearing that, do we?" Phoebe asked Annie, who shook her head, apparently perplexed by the interest in the hair ornament.

Rex picked up his neglected cup of tea. "You had a German au pair working here for a spell, you told me. A student at the university."

"Michaela, yes. But that was before I bought the new mattress. And she had short, spiky hair. In any case, I don't see her wearing something like that. She was very trendy in her dress."

Evidently, Phoebe had been giving the new clue a great deal of thought.

"And that's not all," she declared in triumph.

"Shall I go?" asked the housekeeper, who had been standing by patiently.

"Oh. Yes, Annie. Thank you. I'll take the tray down later." Phoebe returned her attention to Rex. "I found a rounded bit of latex that might have come off a glove. It could be from the tip of one of the fingers. It was in Dad's desk drawer and has a speck of nail polish on it. She might have left her fingerprint on the inside. Is that possible?"

"Aye. Or else some epithelial cells."

"Perhaps the glove got ripped when she scaled the wall or entered the window."

"What did you do with the remnant?" Rex asked.

"It's still in the drawer upstairs. The unlocked drawer. I can't believe I overlooked it before, but it's only a small scrap of clear plastic. Dad kept some financial papers in there. They all seem to be in order. I think I should notify the police, don't you? The young constable I reported the stolen items to seemed sympathetic."

"It's still not a lot to go on," Rex said, adding, "But it's more than we had before."

He would have to look more closely at the female felons in his suspect file, especially the younger ones. Like Phoebe, he could not envision a woman much over forty wearing such a clasp in her hair, and the last case the judge had tried was over ten years ago.

Phoebe sighed with satisfaction as she took a scone from the serving plate. "If nothing else, I feel vindicated. I was afraid you might think me hysterical for asking you down here before."

"Not at all," Rex assured her with more conviction than he had hitherto felt. It was true that he had doubted her motives. "I can't stay beyond tomorrow morning, though," he told her. "My fiancée is expecting me in Derby. She was going to spend the weekend in Edinburgh, but this way we still get to see each other."

Phoebe's downturned mouth turned down even more. "That's a shame. I enjoyed our outing last Sunday so much. I had planned for us to drive to Whitstable for a walk on the beach and lunch at the Old Neptune Pub. Whitstable's a lovely little fishing village with white-washed houses and an old manor house. Peter Cushing lived in Whitstable; you know, the actor in the horror films. Doug used to love those, for some reason."

Rex smiled apologetically at her. "Perhaps next time. How aboot I take you to dinner instead?"

Phoebe's face brightened at once. "All right." She hesitated. "Annie got us some Dover sole. Oh, I suppose it can keep. And she baked a gooseberry pie."

"Give her the night off," Rex suggested. "Perhaps we can have the pie when we get back. I certainly wouldn't want to miss that. Where would you like to go?"

While Phoebe took off to tell the housekeeper about the change of plan, Rex went to freshen up in the bathroom at the top of the stairs in preparation for dinner.

"Shall we walk or take the car?" she asked upon re-joining him in the drawing room.

"Walking would be my preference. It'll feel good to stretch my legs after so many hours on the train."

"It will do me the world of good too. You'll like Burgate, if you haven't already seen it. And we can take a look at Mercery Lane while we're there. It's one of the most picturesque streets in Canterbury."

"Please, lead on," Rex said with a bow.

They donned their coats in the hallway.

"I told Annie to have one of the Dover soles for her supper," Phoebe said.

"Talking of Dover, any news of the missing girl, Lindsay Poulson? I've been busy in court all week and decided to relax with a book on the train, so I'm not well up on the news."

"No developments on that front, sadly. But I suppose until they find a body there's still hope." Phoebe checked her reflection in the hall mirror. "Wouldn't it be awful if they never found out what happened to her?"

A parent's worst nightmare, thought Rex. Fortunately, he was not the one responsible for finding the girl. That task required manpower and massive resources. He fervently prayed the police would make headway.

They walked up to the High Street and ten minutes later reached Burgate, the site of one of the fortified Roman gates once forming part of the city wall. Its street boasted shops and eateries of every description embedded among architecturally diverse buildings from eras gone by. The couple reserved a table at the busy fusion cuisine restaurant Phoebe had chosen and then wandered over to Mercery Lane, where the overhung houses in the narrow medieval street stood crammed and crooked in the shadow of the cathedral towers.

"I can almost believe myself back in the Middle Ages," Rex marvelled, looking about him.

Phoebe nodded in enthusiastic agreement. "Canterbury has a very layered history, just like Edinburgh. That's probably why I feel at home here ... or did. Do you think Annie will be all right alone at the house? Should I install a complete alarm system?"

"It would make you feel safer," Rex suggested, wondering why she had not done so before.

NINETEEN

THE NEXT MORNING AT Phoebe's urging, Rex talked by phone with the constable whom she had contacted about the stolen stamp album and watch. He explained that Mrs. Wells now had reason to believe her father had been murdered.

"Murdered?" Police Constable Bryant asked incredulously.

"She was hesitant to jump to conclusions upon finding the items gone, but now foreign objects have been discovered, further attesting to an intruder's presence in the house and, most importantly, at her father's bedside."

"And what objects might those be, sir?"

"A hair clasp that doesn't belong to any of the household and what appears to be the tip of a latex glove, which was found in one of the desk drawers in the deceased's room. I bagged up the evidence and wondered if you might come to the house?"

The constable agreed, but Rex could tell he was not persuaded there had been a murder, no matter how eager the young copper might be that one had been committed.

When he arrived, Phoebe brought him into the drawing room, where he sat bolt upright in the armchair she offered, his bobby's helmet tucked between knobbly knees.

Rex asked him about the mugging on St. Dunstan's Terrace several weeks ago.

"Nothing new as yet. A random act of violence, we think." The young policeman accepted with thanks a cup of tea and piece of shortbread from the housekeeper.

"I've seen youths loitering on the streets," Annie told him. "I keep my handbag under my coat so no one can grab it."

"Very sensible," the constable said courteously.

Annie finished serving and left the room.

"Can those things be tested for DNA?" Phoebe asked, indicating the two transparent airtight bags Rex had procured from the kitchen and which now lay on the coffee table. As she extended her fingers, Rex could not help but notice that the shade of red on her nails was a match for the varnish on the latex glove, but the sample was so microscopic as to make an exact comparison difficult.

"I'll have to talk to my superiors," Constable Bryant replied around a mouthful of shortbread, which he quickly swallowed. "They may say it's not a strong enough case to warrant a lab test, especially if the death certificate shows nothing amiss."

Rex had expected such a reaction, but had wanted Phoebe to hear it for herself. Now he might wash his hands of the whole business. He really could not see what else he could do unless his friend Thaddeus in London came up with compelling evidence that an old enemy of the judge had been present in Kent to commit murder.

"But," Phoebe said, addressing the constable, "how else could those items have found their way into my father's bed and desk

drawer? My housekeeper uses thick yellow rubber gloves for cleaning. And what about the unlocked window?"

"Circumstantial," the policeman apologized. "I'll try to get someone to take a look, but I can't promise anything."

"Well, that's that," Phoebe said in a disappointed tone after he
had left. "Unless you can come up with anything." She looked at Rex
hopefully.

"I am working on something, but it's a long shot, I'm afraid."

"Oh, well. Thank you for trying."

Annie came in to collect the tea things.

"I don't think anything will come of your discovery," Phoebe
told her.

"Ye did yer best, Mrs. Wells. Ye'll make yourself ill if ye keep on,
and then where will ye be?"

Phoebe sighed deeply. "I suppose you're right, Annie. If Dad
were here now he would probably say the same thing. There may be
a perfectly innocent explanation for a hair clasp being in the bed."

"There now, there may be," the housekeeper consoled her, and
carried out the tray.

"I take it you took her into your confidence," Rex said to Phoebe.

"Up to a point, though not about Dad's murder."

Rex felt awkward making his excuses to leave, but he had done
his best, and he had Helen to think about. He went upstairs and rang
her to let her know he was leaving Canterbury on the next train to
London, and then on to Derby. However, as he was getting his be-
longings together, Phoebe dropped another bombshell after calling
him downstairs to her father's old room.

TWENTY

"I HADN'T NOTICED THE wig's disappearance before," Phoebe said with a panicked look in her dark eyes as she stood before the carved wardrobe positioned perpendicular to the window. Beside it, an oval-mirrored dressing table displayed fabric samples fanned out across its gleaming mahogany surface.

"It was the one your father wore in court?" Rex asked from inside the bedroom doorway.

"Yes, a ratty old thing. I don't know why he kept it. Or why he never bought a new one when he was on the bench. It's not as though he couldn't afford to replace it."

"When you find a comfortable wig, it's hard to part with, and they're not cheap by anyone's standard. I should probably change mine. Where did he keep it?"

"On the top shelf. The head's still there," Phoebe added. "Do you have a head for yours?"

"I do. It helps keep the wig's shape."

"I think wigs are rather silly myself. I can't understand why they're still worn in this country."

"It's part of the tradition. It lends gravitas to the important business of justice."

Phoebe sighed in desperation. "Well, anyway, it's not there, but I can't remember when I last saw it."

"Did you look in the wardrobe when you were searching for the stamp album and watch?"

"No, it only contains old clothes. I looked in it just now because I was going to sort through the contents to see if there was anything I could donate to Oxfam. The crimped spaniel wig Dad wore for ceremonies is still in its box. It's just the bench wig that's gone."

Rex strode to the wardrobe to see for himself. As Phoebe had stated, a bare moulded plastic head and neck stood rather macabrely on the top shelf. "Perhaps your father got rid of it."

"Why would he suddenly decide to do that after all these years?"

"I don't know. It's very peculiar. Especially in light of the other missing items." Rex wondered why a thief would steal a worn-out old wig. "There may be some reasonable explanation," he said, "Though it eludes me for now."

Phoebe smiled. "Yes, it's all a bit of a brain-teaser, isn't it? If our intruder used a clasp, she must have had hair and wouldn't have needed a wig." She giggled and clamped a hand to her mouth. "Sorry, it's nerves."

Or booze, Rex couldn't help but wonder. "Perhaps the judge had a secret paramour." He chuckled.

Phoebe laughed along with him, which made her face look almost girlish, her black eyes shiny as liquorice. "Somehow I don't think so."

Rex's hand coursed through the hangars in the wardrobe, which exuded a woodsy scent laced with lavender. Among the deceased's clothes, and swathed in plastic, hung the judge's red cape, faced with red crosses, over a white-trimmed red robe. "Well, let's consider the other possibilities," he said. "Are you sure there isn't anything else you've missed?"

"Pretty sure. Should I report the old wig as stolen too?" she asked with a straight face.

Rex shrugged. "I suppose so. I do find it strange that only personal items are missing and nothing of greater value."

"There's nothing of value in here, apart from some of Dad's books, and they'd be too heavy to carry out of a window. The burglar can't have left the room or she would have found several antiques and ornaments downstairs."

"You're sure none of your jewellery was taken?"

"Absolutely sure. And thank goodness. She'd have had to come in my room while I was asleep, which I would have been in the early hours of the morning." Phoebe looked frightened. "The thought of a stranger creeping around my bedroom is thoroughly terrifying."

"And there's no lock on your bedroom door, correct?" he asked.

"There is now. I had Alan Burke install one of those sliding bolts on Monday, that locks on the inside."

Rex nodded. "Did your handyman ask why you were taking the extra security measure?"

"No. It's not that unusual, is it? With me alone here with Annie ... And he had to replace a washer in the kitchen tap, which had started to drip."

Rex told her she had done the right thing putting in the bolt. "What's in that box?" he asked, gazing at the top shelf of the wardrobe.

"Dad's ceremonial wig."

"Did you search behind it?" Better to find out now than to be called back later, he decided.

"No, I couldn't reach."

Rex groped around the back of the shelf and rummaged beneath the piles of clothing. He touched an envelope, which he pulled out and examined.

It was a rather old envelope, judging by the discoloured paper, and was addressed to Gordon Murgatroyd at Phoebe's residence. Three abbreviated wavy black marks showed where postage had been affixed.

He turned over the envelope. The flap had been opened, leaving a few ragged tears, and resealed.

"I wonder who it's from," murmured Phoebe beside him. "And why isn't it with Dad's other correspondence?"

He handed it to her. "Why don't you open it and see?"

Phoebe ran a red fingernail under the flap, which gave away easily, and drew out a single sheet of notepaper. "It's in German," she stated. "Looks like a woman wrote it. I can't make out her name. Perhaps if I got my glasses."

Rex fished his out of the pocket of his trousers and put them on. "Permit me. Not that my German is up to much, especially when it's written in longhand."

The letter was confined to one side of the page. "It's addressed affectionately to your father and signed 'Veronika.'"

"I don't know a Veronika. What does it say?"

Rex perused the note, barely able to make it out, but it mentioned the word *Tochter* a couple of times and the name Elvie.

"Elvie is doing well at her university in Stuttgart," he translated aloud.

"Who's Elvie?"

"'Our daughter'. I think that's what it says."

"No idea who that might be."

"Did your father ever go to Germany?"

"He visited Munich a few times while he was still living in Edinburgh. This was over twenty years ago. I think the trips had something to do with stamps. He was gone for a couple of weeks."

"There's no sender's address. The letter must be important if he kept it. It's dated five years ago." Rex refolded the sheet and returned it to its envelope. "Perhaps your father misplaced it after removing the stamps. I could take it with me and have someone give us a proper translation."

Phoebe shrugged. "Fine, but it's probably nothing. He must have forgotten about it. Over the past five years it would have been almost impossible for him to get at the envelope, tall as he was. He had started to lose range of motion by then. Even you had to reach up."

The light dust on his fingers suggested the shelf had not been cleaned in a while. He further wondered if he would find cobwebs on top of the wardrobe. He had difficulty imagining the elderly housekeeper balancing on a step ladder.

He suddenly remembered the time and went back up to his room to grab his bag before anything else came up to delay him. Phoebe drove him to the train station, talking about the hidden letter and racking her brains as to who might have sent it.

He called Helen from his mobile as soon as he reached the platform. "A short delay, but I'm on my way," he announced. He told her what time to expect him at the station in Derby.

"Any further developments with the case?" she asked.

"Hard to say. The police may deem the evidence too flimsy to proceed with. And to be truthful, I'm not sure what to think myself. But Phoebe seemed more calm and resigned when I left her."

"That's good," his fiancée said. "And what would you like to do with the rest of your weekend?"

"Just spend it with you, quietly at home."

"I was hoping you'd say that," Helen told him with a smile in her voice.

TWENTY-ONE

THAT EVENING AFTER A quiet dinner at Helen's home, Rex lay content and relaxed beside her on the sofa. With her blonde hair, blue eyes, and a mouth prone to smiling, she was the antithesis of Phoebe Wells. His fiancée probed his neck with gentle fingers. A few tell-tale yellow marks remained of the bruising, easily covered up when he wore a shirt with a high collar, which was now open.

"Don't say it," he warned with a smile.

"What?"

"That I should be more careful."

"Well, you should. Especially after last time."

Clearly she was referring to the case a while back in Bedfordshire, where he had narrowly escaped with his life. "I came back in one piece then just as I did this time," he pointed out.

She tapped his bearded jaw. "Next time you might not be so lucky."

"Well, I'm letting the police take care of Dan Sutter, if they can find him."

"And what about the judge's murderer?" Helen asked. "If he exists."

"Right." Rex stretched out his arms and yawned. "And it is a big 'if'. No sign of forced entry and nothing taken outside the bedroom. Possibly the intruder was scared off."

"Scared off by what? You said only Phoebe was at home and that she didn't hear anything. Maybe there was nothing to hear. Maybe she hid the album and wristwatch herself, and now the wig, to give her an excuse to get you down there."

Rex had kept Helen apprised of every step in the case. "If that's true," he said, "it's quite an elaborate plan."

"Not really. I wonder what she'll come up with next?"

"So you're not prepared to give her the benefit of the doubt?" he asked, raising his eyebrows at her and smiling.

"I might if it weren't so obvious she was after you."

Rex shook his head pensively. "She told me aboot the missing album during our first phone call. I hadn't seen her in over ten years and I don't recall us ever having had a proper conversation. We just happened to be at some of the same social functions her father was attending."

"Well, no doubt you made an impression on her, and then when you called to offer your condolences, she saw her chance, her being a widow now and probably having heard that you were widowed."

Rex scratched his ear in puzzlement. "She does not strike me as a scheming woman. If anything, she's a wee bit doolally."

"An act," Helen teased.

Rex saw that his fiancée was not being completely serious, and yet in all truth, the same thoughts had occurred to him. "Well, if Phoebe is not making it all up, I may be looking for a female housebreaker. It would not have taken much force to subdue an old man and suffocate him with a pillow. Forensic testing might reveal prints on the hair ornament or scrap of latex linking them to a known offender."

Helen laughed and tossed her abundant blonde hair back from her face. "I'm sorry, but I'm trying to picture it: a young woman smothering an octogenarian for a stamp album, an old watch, and a scruffy old wig. If she was interrupted in her diabolical actions, why even bother with those things? She'd be out the window and away as fast as her murderous legs could carry her."

Rex got the impression from Helen's sardonic tone that, not only did she mistrust Phoebe's intentions, she no doubt felt resentful because she and Rex had not been able to spend the whole weekend together. He decided the best thing would be to drop the discussion altogether.

"And then there's the letter," she added before he could do so. "Were you meant to find that?"

"I won't know until I know what it says."

He would have to find someone competent enough in German to render an accurate translation on the off chance the mysterious missive provided a clue in this most peculiar case.

TWENTY-TWO

That Monday morning, Rex knocked on Alistair's door and poked his head inside the office, where his colleague sat behind his desk busily clicking away on his laptop.

"Sorry to interrupt, but how's your German?" Rex enquired.

"Nine goot, I'm afraid. Why?"

"I discovered an old letter squirreled away in Gordon Murgatroyd's wardrobe. It's from a woman in Germany and mentions a daughter at university in Stuttgart. It refers to 'our' daughter, and there's a long word I don't recognize with the word for daughter in it. The letter is personal in tone, and I thought it might be pertinent to my investigation."

"A love letter to Judge Murder? About a love child? Why, the old goat!"

"He was a pillar of rectitude and, as far as I knew, faithful to his late wife's memory," Rex remonstrated.

"How can you be such an idealist, Rex, when you see the worst of human nature every day in our profession? Even judges can deviate from the straight and narrow, you know. And he was a widower, after all, just like yourself." Alistair reached out his hand. "Leave it with me. I know a native German court interpreter. I'll let you know as soon as it's been translated."

Rex gave Alistair the envelope with his profound thanks and hurried off to attend to court business.

During the course of the day, he found himself turning over the letter in his mind. Did Judge Murgatroyd really have another daughter? He would likely have made some provision for her in his will if that were the case, and Phoebe had told him her father had left everything to her. Rex could not reconcile the stern judge in his wig and gown withholding the secret of a half-sister from Phoebe.

Late in the afternoon, he visited Pruitt in hospital to deliver the books he had promised. The patient was wearing a pair of black-framed glasses and what looked to be his own pyjamas instead of a hospital gown. The sticking plaster on his neck had shrunk in size, and he had more colour in his round face and bald, egg-shaped head.

"Sorry to be getting back to you so late, but I had to go to Canterbury." Rex placed the reading material on the narrow bed and grabbed a chair. "I took the liberty of bringing you a book from Canterbury and also what you asked for."

Pruitt thanked him for the handsome tome on Scottish history and eagerly leafed through the glossy pages of photographs.

"How have you been?" Rex asked.

"Bored, mostly. My fellow patients are not a lively lot, as you can see. And there's constant interruption which prevents me from sleeping, what with doctors' rounds, nurses coming in for this and that at all hours, and a stream of visitors—though not for me."

"I think the police are rigorously monitoring who sees you. It took a bit of persuading before I was let in."

"Oh, that could be it," Pruitt said, letting out his breath. "Better safe than sorry, eh? Dan Sutter is a devious and dangerous man. Any news on that front?"

"He's still evading the long arm of the law. The police are searching for him far away from here."

"I heard." Pruitt furrowed his brow. "He must be desperate. I don't think he has family in northwest Scotland."

"You said you had retained the services of a private investigator. Presumably you have information on Sutter's background?"

"I do. It's not a stellar background. Grew up poor, left school early, in and oot of Borstal for theft, and then ten years inside for breaking into that house with a weapon."

"Can you elaborate on that if it does not hurt too much to speak?" Pruitt's voice sounded a bit stronger, though it still held the reedy quality Rex remembered from their first phone conversation.

"My throat's much better. I'm being discharged tomorrow. The wound will leave a scar, but it won't be too noticeable when I wear a bow tie. It will all be worth it if Dan Sutter is caught and confesses to abducting and murdering April Showers." Pruitt smiled with satisfaction. "Then everyone will be sorry they never believed me." He paused. "Where were we ...? Aye, the lesser charge Sutter went down for, instead of attempted assault on a minor ..."

He reached for his beaker and took a protracted sip of water while Rex waited. Clearly the man had a flair for the dramatic, as he recalled from the media coverage ten years ago. Pruitt carefully replaced his plastic cup by his bedside and began to speak again.

"It couldn't be proved that it was other than a bungled house break-in. Sutter jumped from the window and broke his ankle. He only managed to cover a short distance before being picked up near Holyrood Park. Swore he had no idea one of the occupants of the house was a young girl. He said the knife in his possession was for forcing open windows and the rope was for scaling walls." Pruitt drank some more water.

"What proof do you have that he was involved in April Showers' abduction and murder?" Rex probed.

"The similarity between the two crimes and the timing," Pruitt replied. "And the fact they occurred within the city centre. I have a map pinpointing the crime scenes."

Rex remained less than convinced. For one thing, April Showers had been snatched off the street, as he recalled, and not from her home. Pruitt's theory was based purely on supposition. "Be that as it may," he told the patient, "Sutter tried to kill you and put you in hospital. That's serious enough to get him locked up for a good long time."

Rex looked about him at the sterile surroundings and bedridden bodies. "I'm sure you'll be glad to leave this place." Even visiting for short periods left him depressed.

"I'll say. I hate the hospital smell. It pervades the food, especially the scrambled eggs. I think they're made with powder," Pruitt confided. "Still, I can't help but worry about going home. The police have offered me some measure of protection, but they can't watch over me forever."

"It looks like Sutter is long gone," Rex tried to calm Pruitt, who had become agitated in his movements and had spilt water on his top sheet. "Where did your investigator follow him?"

"To the dole office, to a support group for the jobless, thrift shops, cheap food chains. Sutter didn't visit family, and there was no girlfriend in the picture. He frequented a couple of seedy pubs where he liked to play darts. All in all, he was keeping his nose clean, until he came after me. Glover, the PI, has cost me a bundle and look where it got me."

Pruitt looked woebegone in his hospital bed. Now that he was on the road to recovery, his mind was clearly concerned with his uncertain future. And Rex could not blame him. Dan Sutter had amply demonstrated his violent nature. His own mind would not rest easy until the man had been apprehended.

TWENTY-THREE

ALISTAIR SWUNG BY REX'S office early on Tuesday afternoon with the German letter and its typed translation.

Rex read it with interest and nodded. "I'll tell Phoebe."

"So what's new on your private case?" Alistair asked, seating himself in the chair across the desk from Rex and elegantly crossing his long legs, clad in immaculate pinstripe trousers.

"Not much at this point. I can't go after Sutter in the wilds of nowhere, but I can look into his past."

"What for? It's got nothing to do with Judge M's murder. Or, rather, Phoebe Wells screaming blue murder."

"Richard Pruitt is convinced Sutter attacked April Showers and dumped her body in Skinner's Close. I'm inclined to believe Pruitt didn't do those things, which means no one has been brought to justice in the girl's murder. Her parents no doubt assume Pruitt got away with it, just like everyone else does. So now there are two wrongs to right: an innocent man falsely accused and a guilty man who walks free, whether it be Sutter or somebody else."

"But you can't take that old case on, Rex," Alistair argued, leaning forward with his arms draped over his lap. "See if you can get the police to look into it."

"And have them admit they got the wrong man?" Rex shook his head. "I don't have enough proof yet. Make that any proof, other than Pruitt's suspicions."

"A man with a vested interest in blaming someone else and exonerating himself," Alistair pointed out.

"Well, I'd want to be exonerated if I'd been charged with something I didn't do. You should have seen him in hospital, Alistair. He looked so pitiful and alone."

"I know, you big softie. I went to visit him this morning. He sent me a note, saying he wanted to thank me in person for saving his life."

Rex felt a wide grin spread over his face. "I'm so glad you went, Alistair. He's not had many visitors."

"I said it was on the express condition he didn't talk about me to reporters. I don't want them hounding me. It's not as though I did anything heroic, just what any reasonable human being would do."

"Did he talk aboot Sutter?"

"Naturally. He's scared witless."

"Perhaps we could visit him at home one day this week and make sure he's all right."

"Don't you have enough going on here?"

Rex glanced at his tidy desk. "Not so far. I wrapped up my case on Friday, if you recall."

"I do, and I owe you a drink."

"I'll gladly take you up on that, but it can't be this evening. I've arranged to meet Stu Showers."

Alistair gave a start. "Stu Showers? You mean, the murdered girl's father?"

"I need details on his daughter's murder that might shed light on the perpetrator."

"And he's willing to talk to you after the Crown failed him by not locking Pruitt up?" Alistair asked in surprise.

"He won't talk to me in his wife's presence. He's coming alone. He said he sat through the trial and could not blame the jury for returning the verdict they did. He didn't think the police had done a thorough enough job of pinning evidence on Pruitt. Anyway, he says he just wants to know the truth, either way. That's another reason I want to go back to Ramsay Garden. I need to see what solid evidence Pruitt might have on Dan Sutter."

Alistair raised an immaculate eyebrow. "I'd think, if there was something truly significant, he'd have told you. He was gabby enough with me, for someone who had his throat cut a week ago."

"Well, I thought I'd give him time to settle in at home before I prod him further. In the meantime I need to discover what I can from Mr. Showers. He knows the case as well as anyone and he knew his daughter better than most. I just can't let this go, Alistair."

His friend sighed in resignation. "I can see that, and I know what an obstinate mule you are. But don't go back to Ramsay Garden without me. Dan Sutter may be hiding in some remote croft on a godforsaken island, or he may not. Richard told me the police found a map of the Hebrides in Sutter's rubbish bin, but don't you think he would have taken it with him if he was going there?"

This gave Rex pause. DCI Lauper had not mentioned to him how he had managed to locate Sutter's whereabouts. "You think he was intentionally misleading the police?"

"Why not? Let's not assume the man's a fool, especially if he managed to get away with April's murder."

"Well, she *was* stabbed, and he attacked you and Pruitt with a knife and threatened me with one. He had a knife on him when he was found escaping from the house he said he'd only been in to steal from. Young girl, knife..." Rex clicked his pen open and shut with his thumb as he spoke, thinking it through. "And both incidents did take place in the heart of Edinburgh within six months of each other. Pruitt claims there's a pattern. It's a tenuous one, granted, but the more I dwell on it..."

"If you wish to pursue it, that's enough for me. You have my full support."

"Thank you, Alistair."

Rex had a feeling he would need it.

TWENTY-FOUR

STU SHOWERS HAD REQUESTED they meet at a chip shop on Rose Street in New Town. Rex's first impression upon seeing April's father was that he looked older than a man of forty-five should. His face had the grey tinge and rigid lines of a hardened smoker and he sat hunched inside a nylon jacket, although it was not cold inside the cramped premises redolent of fish, curry, and grease.

The chip shop catered to students and the working poor. Showers apparently belonged to the latter, as indicated by his accent and manner of speech and by his clean but worn clothes.

As he and Rex made small talk at a window booth, Rex could not help but notice his companion's disfigured hand on the table, clearly the result of an accident rather than some birth defect. A surgeon had attempted to save what remained of a thumb and forefinger, that its owner might retain some functionality from the mangled extremity. The remaining three fingers had been shorn off at the first joint.

A pimply youth brought their tea in a metal pot accompanied by a smaller one of milk and two cups and saucers made of cheap green china. Showers used his right hand to push the cup and saucer to his left side. He poured proficiently enough, though it was apparent he was not born left-handed and had not had a lifetime to adjust to his disability.

"As I explained on the phone," he told Rex, "Pauline would only be upset if she knew I was raking up the past. She turned to religion to help get her through our loss. I just want to know the truth. Are you looking at someone in particular?"

Rex swallowed a mouthful of strong tea. "I'm only at the beginning of my inquiry, but I am following a particular lead. What I was hoping for from you were details regarding your daughter and anything you heard at Richard Pruitt's trial that might be helpful in identifying an alternate perpetrator. If it's not too upsetting for you."

Showers shrugged slightly and nodded. "I can try if you think it'll help. We've got to get these predators off the street. There's that girl gone missing in England. Lindsay Poulson. The police have nothing, or the news would have kept up with the story. She's around the same age my April was. Preying on children," he added, raising his maimed hand to his mouth and shaking his head. "It's beyond my understanding."

He went on to admit he had been tempted to go after Pruitt at first simply because he needed someone to take his rage out on, but had just returned to work at the bottling plant after a leave of compassion when his hand was caught in a machine. "I lost my concentration for a split second. My mind just wasna on the job. I was in hospital for a month and now I'm on permanent disability."

"Can you walk me through the circumstances of your daughter's disappearance, Stu?"

Showers took a sip from his precariously full cup of tea and carefully set it back down in the saucer. "April walked her friend home after school and was making her way to our place when she was taken. Kate and her mum said she had left well before dark. No one saw her after that. It's a fifteen-minute walk from Kate's flat on Lothian Road to ours in Lauriston Place."

Rex nodded thoughtfully. He had studied the central city route the girl took to walk to and from school. Lothian Road ran from the west end of Princes Street south to Tollcross, where the Showers family lived. A bustling thoroughfare of shops, nail spas, pubs, clubs, and restaurants, it was home to the Caledonian, built at the turn of the last century as a Grand Railway Hotel and notable for its size and red sandstone façade. All in all, an unlikely setting for an abduction, Rex thought. And no one had seen anything suspicious in Lauriston Place, according to archived newspaper stories he had read.

"Any short-cuts she might have taken?" he asked Showers.

"None that would have made any sense."

"No other friends she might have stopped by to visit?"

"She rang her ma from Kate's to say she'd be home right after tea. It took a while for my wife to stop blaming herself. She says if only she'd gone to fetch April ... We don't own a car and April only took the bus when it was snowing or raining. Pauline had a cleaning job and arranged it so she'd always be home before April. She was our only bairn and Pauline was verra protective," Showers ended in a sob.

"Things can happen whatever precautions you take," Rex consoled the bereaved man. He gave him a minute to compose himself. "From what I've read, April was in school clothes. Black pleated skirt, and a dark fleece jacket. Is that correct?"

"Aye, and I brought photos as you asked." Mr. Showers fumbled with a small zipped binder and opened it midway. He turned it on the table to face Rex and pointed.

Beneath a film of plastic, a dark-haired girl stood with a group of classmates on a day trip to Hadrian's Wall. Another picture showed April made up with purple eyeshadow and blackish lipstick and wearing a clingy top over her undeveloped bust. Her long hair hung loose, worn parted to the side, and she was attempting a pout. No artifice could disguise her thirteen years. Her face had not completely lost its baby fat and her brown eyes were those of a child.

"Someone had to have transported her to Skinner's Close," Showers said.

"Would she have accepted a lift from someone?"

Showers vigorously shook his head. "Pauline went on and on to her aboot never getting into a stranger's car, and it wasna a long walk from Kate's. There'd be no reason to."

"A family member?"

"Both our families, Pauline's and mine, are in Glasgow. And April's friends were not old enough to drive. I went through all this with the detectives." Showers sagged over his cup of tea.

"I know. But I wanted to hear it from you, so I could form my own impressions."

"They even thought I might have had something to do with it. My own daughter!"

"They have to consider everybody as a potential suspect," Rex told him, "starting with those closest to the victim. Can I offer you something to eat?"

The frail man looked in dire need of sustenance. He shook his head, and then changed his mind. Rex ordered chips with curry sauce for two. When the food arrived in the shallow cartons, he realized just how hungry he was, having eaten only a sandwich for lunch at his desk.

"Very good curry," he remarked to Showers, who seemed pleased by the QC's approval.

"Wasna sure how you'd feel aboot meeting at a chippy. Pauline's working late. She has her own cleaning company now. I said I'd fend for myself."

They ate for a few moments in silence, and then Showers shook his head briefly. "I watched Richard Pruitt in court. I just couldna picture him pushing our April into a car on a busy street withoot drawing attention. She was lippy; at that age where she'd even started talking back to her mother. She was small, but she would have fought back and shouted, 'Get off me, ye wee perv!' or something like that. No, Pruitt didna strike me as an aggressive man. Odd, aye. No doubt aboot that. But timid."

Rex tended to agree. However, he had prosecuted meek men in his career, and often they were the ones most prone to preying on weaker victims.

"And the defence made quite a bit aboot the fact April's clothes reeked of Old Spice, which Pruitt claimed he never wore," Showers continued. "And I couldna see him wearing that."

It was remotely possible April's body had lain in spilt aftershave, Rex conceded, or else an emergency worker at the crime scene handling her in an official capacity had gone overboard with it in preparation for a night out. Yet common sense dictated it probably belonged to the killer.

"There was a load of other rubbish that came up in court," Showers went on to remark.

"That's the other reason I wanted to talk to you. I haven't read the court transcripts, but you were at the trial."

"Every day, painful as it was." Showers took in a deep breath. "And it never really goes away."

Whoever April's killer was, Rex vowed to himself to find out the truth. Her father had not become bitter in spite of all the misfortune that had befallen him, and at the very least he deserved answers.

On the subject of answers, he made a point to call Phoebe as soon as he got home and relayed the contents of the letter from Veronika in Germany.

"So Elvie is Dad's goddaughter?" she recapped. "I wonder ... I've been trying to think of any German people he knew. He was evacuated during the war with a boy who had escaped Nazi Germany with his family. I believe they kept in touch until Herman died. I'll see if I can find him in Dad's address book. Veronika might be his wife. Elvie might not know her godfather passed away. I'm sure Dad would have left her something if he'd been of sounder mind when he revised his last will and testament three years ago. He became so very forgetful. I could write and send her some money on his behalf at the university where she works."

"That would be a nice gesture," Rex said, knowing that Phoebe, by her own admission, had plenty to spare.

However, the letter did not bring them closer to discovering who might have murdered the judge.

TWENTY-FIVE

THE NEXT DAY, REX went back to Ramsay Garden, where a patrol car was parked in front of the entrance leading to the flat. Two policemen sat inside and one got out as Rex approached.

"Richard Pruitt is expecting me."

"Your name, sir."

"Rex Graves QC."

"I'll need to see some identity, please."

Rex showed him his driving licence. "Are you here around the clock?" he asked.

"When he's home, yes, sir. You may go up."

"Thank you."

Rex pressed the buzzer and Pruitt's voice answered, sounding more robust than in hospital. Rex announced himself and made his way up the narrow stone steps to the terrace. Pruitt greeted him at the door with a beaming smile.

"Glad you could make it," he said. He was dressed in a pair of pressed slacks, a lime-green shirt, and a paisley-patterned bow tie.

Rex noted a subtle scent of cologne on his person when he shook his hand. "I was just making a gin and tonic. Can I tempt you?"

"By all means." Rex removed his coat in the hall and hung it up on a polished mahogany rack aligned with brass hooks. "Everything looks back in order here."

"I've been busy cleaning. One feels so violated when one's home is broken into. Two of my rings went missing from my bedroom, a carnelian and an onyx, each in a beautiful silver setting."

"Did you report it to the police?"

"Naturally, and to my insurance company. I have more valuable stuff he could have pinched, but I suppose he took a fancy to them."

"He was wearing two rings when I saw him. One had a reddish stone, the other was black, I think."

"The gall of the man! And I'll have to re-carpet the guest cupboard to get rid of the blood stains. Sorry aboot the smell of bleach. It's not as noticeable in the sitting room."

With a flutter in his stomach, Rex surveyed the window seat, where he had succumbed to his torment. The shades were lifted, revealing the landscaped gardens reserved for residents. He could also see the squad car, a reassuring sight, as he imagined it must be for Pruitt.

"Alistair was held up in court, but he'll be along shortly to see you," Rex told him as he accepted his gin and tonic. His colleague would have dissuaded him from coming alone were it not for the police presence Pruitt had been able to confirm.

"Excellent. I prepared some hors-d'oeuvres. It was such a luxury to be able to run to Marks and Spencer and stock up on food after the dreadful slop I was served in hospital."

"I'm sure. While we're waiting for Alistair, perhaps I can review any records on Dan Sutter you can show me."

"Certainly. Make yourself comfortable while I fetch them. I keep them in a shoebox in the attic. But don't tell anyone." Pruitt put a finger to his lips and set down his drink on an end table.

Shortly after his host left the room, Rex heard a creaking sound, and then the clang of metal, presumably a ladder being pulled down to access the attic. It sounded as though the noises were coming from the guest bedroom where Alistair had found Pruitt's almost lifeless body. Rex had been too woozy at the time to notice an attic. And then he heard a muted scream.

He rushed to the floral-papered room just as Pruitt scrambled down the ladder descending from a trap door. He missed a rung in his haste and slipped, landing with a jolt on the carpet.

"It's gone," he squeaked, his face a white mask.

"The shoebox? Are you sure?"

Pruitt did not answer. He simply stared at Rex through his black-framed glasses.

"What's the matter, Richard?" Surely Sutter could not be hiding in the attic, or else Pruitt would not still be standing there.

"You'd better take a look and see for yourself." Pruitt spoke as though his throat had gone dry.

Rex felt disinclined to look, if Pruitt's shocked expression was anything to go by, and gazed up with trepidation into the sloped roof cavity.

"You'll see from the top of the ladder. It's not an attic you can get all the way into. I just use it for storage."

And for stuff you don't want other people to find, Rex thought. And yet it seemed someone had found Pruitt's shoebox.

He braced himself for the ascent. The flimsy ladder groaned under his weight. "Is this thing securely attached?" he asked.

"Aye, just watch your head on the rafter. There's no headroom, except for a decapitated one."

Rex proceeded with slow, deliberate steps. As soon as his head cleared the opening he froze. He thought he must be hallucinating. Pruitt had not been joking about a decapitated head.

"Do you see it?" he called from below.

"Hard to miss." Rex realized he was gripping the ladder so tight the metal was digging into his palms.

"What's it doing there?" Pruitt wailed. "Why would he put a woman's skull in my attic? It's still got hair, with blood, on it," he faltered, and made a gagging sound.

"You think Sutter put it here?" Rex asked, peering at the object. "Is there a light?"

"Pull on the string to your left."

A single naked bulb cast illumination into the small attic.

"Who else could it be?" Pruitt demanded. "He took my research on him."

"It's only a papier-mâché skull," Rex said, viewing it clearly in the light. "And I'm not sure the blood is real. It's a judge's bench wig."

"A judge's wig? Not human hair?"

"Definitely not. It's horsehair." Stiff and frizzy and yellowed from age, with two dangling ties at the back.

"Well, that's some relief, I suppose."

Rex glanced down and saw Pruitt lift his glasses and mop his face with a handkerchief. "If Sutter did this, when did he, I wonder?"

"When I was in hospital?"

Or earlier today, Rex considered, while Pruitt was shopping for groceries. The police might have decided to take a break in their charge's absence. "How would he have got in?" he asked Pruitt.

"The man's a burglar."

Just then the buzzer sounded, causing Rex to almost lose his balance on the ladder. "See if the police car is still outside," he instructed.

While Pruitt scuttled off, Rex took his phone from his pocket and took photographs of the bewigged head from all angles as best he could without touching it.

"The police are still there," he heard Pruitt call out to him. "Should I answer the buzzer?" he asked just as it sounded again.

"Aye." Rex descended the ladder and entered the hall in time to hear Alistair's voice.

"Get the police up here, will you?" Rex said into the intercom.

When Alistair returned with the two policemen, Rex explained that someone had left Richard a grotesque object in the attic and said he couldn't be sure the intruder wasn't hiding in the flat. Alistair stood at the foot of the ladder while the first constable, a burly fellow, clambered up to the attic.

"There's nowhere really to hide," Pruitt objected as the other officer began flinging open doors and checking under the beds.

"When did you last see the shoebox?" Rex asked Pruitt.

"A day or so before I was taken to hospital."

Rex returned to the guest bedroom, where Alistair stood with the burly constable at the foot of the ladder discussing whether the red smears on the wig could be tested for blood. The constable said he would call in a detective.

"Pete Lauper?" Rex asked.

He was told it would be his subordinate. Chief Inspector Lauper was in Stornoway on the island of Lewis in the Outer Hebrides, where there had been a sighting of Dan Sutter.

"Then Sutter can't have been here very recently," Rex said. And he could not take the policemen to task for being remiss in their guard duty. "Did he have a shoebox with him after he attacked you last Monday?" Rex asked Alistair.

"No, he left empty-handed. Well, apart from the knife."

"He might have returned while I was in hospital," Pruitt repeated.

"Can you get CCTV footage since Mr. Pruitt was attacked?" Rex asked the policemen.

While they questioned Pruitt, Alistair pulled Rex into the hall. "What's the meaning of all this, d'you think?"

Rex shook his head and shrugged. "Richard went to the attic to get information on Sutter. When I went up, I was confronted by what could be Murgatroyd's old wig daubed with red something or other. That's all I know."

"Might be paint or tomato paste," Alistair said. "It's a bit orange to be real blood, but we'll see."

"It looked convincing enough in the dark, I can tell you."

"A bit theatrical, don't you agree? What makes you think it might be Judge M's wig?"

"It could be one just like it," Rex allowed. "From a costume or second-hand shop. But it looks like Murgatroyd's, and his went missing from his daughter's house."

Alistair paced the hall, pivoting suddenly to face Rex. "Is Sutter playing some sort of sick joke? What significance could the wig have for Richard?"

"He remained in contact with Judge Murgatroyd after his trial." Rex folded his arms tightly and frowned. "He's been having Sutter followed by a private investigator. The bloodied wig could be a warning. The question is, how did Sutter get hold of Murgatroyd's wig? If it is, in fact, his?"

Alistair dragged Rex further away from the guest bedroom where Pruitt was giving his statement. "You don't suppose Richard put it in the attic himself?"

"What for?"

"To get attention," Alistair said in hushed tones. "Like Phoebe Wells."

"Phoebe was not stabbed to within an inch of her life. Richard's shock at finding the wig struck me as genuine."

Alistair gave a casual shrug. "I'm just throwing the possibility out there."

"At this point I'm not sure what to think," Rex admitted. "The appearance of a judge's wig opens up a whole Pandora's box of questions."

Alistair clasped Rex on the shoulder. "Cheer up, old fruit. Only the other day you were deploring the fact you had nothing much to go on."

DCI Lauper's partner arrived just then and had Rex and Richard go over their bizarre discovery again. He asked to be filled in on everything pertaining to their interactions with Dan Sutter, and Alistair gave his own account of his run-in with the fugitive.

Detective Inspector Rice made copious notes in a small spiral pad. "I know you've already given DCI Lauper much of this information, but he'll want to be brought up to speed when he gets back."

When he had finished with his questions, he informed Pruitt that the ladder and attic would be dusted for fingerprints. The convalescing man, just one day out of hospital, was distraught to hear the news. "Can you do a better job of cleaning up this time?" he asked querulously.

Rice enquired if there was somewhere else he could stay.

"I feel defeated," Pruitt said, wandering into the kitchen and collapsing onto a chair.

The hors-d'oeuvres he had set out on the table had gone untouched. Alistair kindly offered to take him home with him, and

Pruitt readily agreed. With that settled, Rex went home himself, eager to process the new developments in peace and quiet.

His mother and Miss Bird had a Charitable Ladies' meeting to attend that evening, and his dinner was waiting in the oven. Rex lit a fire in the parlour, opened a bottle of claret, and installed himself with a tray on the sofa. Glass of wine in hand, he began to relax, giving his jumbled thoughts free rein as he gazed into the wavering flames.

The ringing of his phone soon put paid to his reflections. It was Thaddeus calling from London with a promising lead on a felon in the Murgatroyd case.

TWENTY-SIX

THE NEXT DAY, REX met Alistair for a pub lunch in belated celebration of his having won a guilty verdict in his last trial. They had both had a busy morning and this was their first opportunity to discuss the events of the previous evening.

"How is your new house guest?" Rex asked as they grabbed a newly vacated table.

"Richard is fine. He stayed in my basement last night." Alistair occupied a Georgian house in Albany Street in the heart of New Town. "But he's anxious to return to his flat as soon as he gets the all-clear from the police."

"Poor man. He was so happy to be home yesterday. But your basement, Alistair?"

"What's wrong with it? It's luxury accommodation. And since I'm not letting it right now … What?" he asked when Rex did not answer. "You think he should have stayed upstairs with me? Don't worry, I made him my special pasta with portobello mushrooms and scallops and opened a nice bottle of Chablis. I even regaled him with the operas of Verdi's middle period. He's a man of refined taste is our Richard, though a bit cuckoo. I asked him if he'd like to stay in my renovated basement, and he was delighted when I showed it to him. You haven't seen it since it was kitted out with quartz countertops and the latest in chrome fixtures. It would be rated five stars if it was a hotel."

"I just meant he might be frightened on his own."

"He feels he's safe for now, but Detective Inspector Rice told me this morning the sighting on Lewis was false. Dan Sutter could be anywhere. I haven't told Richard yet. I thought I'd give him a reprieve before I deliver this latest bit of bad news. DCI Lauper is headed back to Edinburgh."

A server arrived to clear the empty glasses from the previous customers and wipe down their table. They placed their orders.

"Richard will have to be told before he goes home," Rex said, resuming their conversation after the young man had left. "Pete Lauper won't be pleased to have missed oot on the action yesterday while pursuing a futile search of the Western Isles. What happened up there?"

"The man they tracked down was misidentified by the person who saw the police flyer of Sutter at a post office. The look-alike had the misfortune to be wearing a blue pullover similar to the one Sutter had on the day he attacked us at Ramsay Garden. He was a freelance photographer visiting Lewis and Harris on assignment."

Rex sighed dispiritedly. "Aye, well, someone could easily be mistaken for Dan Sutter. I wonder if he's taken pains to disguise himself. Dyed his hair, grown a beard, be wearing glasses, maybe?"

"Or heels," Alistair said half-seriously.

Rex looked around for their drinks and spotted the young man approaching with them across the heavily populated floor. "So Dan

Sutter is still at large. Not very reassuring. And there's another unsavoury character in the picture."

He told Alistair about the phone call from his associate Thaddeus concerning a name on the shortlist of suspects in Murgatroyd's possible murder. "He discovered a Canterbury connection, and I immediately recognized the name Burke, first name Bruce. Phoebe Wells has a handyman by the name of Alan Burke. Prison records show Alan visiting Bruce at Shotts, thirty miles from here. He's his brother and, apparently, a close one at that to have come all this way. Dan Sutter was an inmate at Shotts. The coincidences just keep mounting."

"You don't believe in coincidences, remember." Alistair thanked the server and picked up his glass of ale. "Seems I misjudged Phoebe. I thought she was making it all up about her father being murdered and things mysteriously disappearing from her house."

Rex took a swig of Guinness. "You accused her of screaming blue murder," he jokingly reminded his friend.

"I eat my words." Alistair reached into the pocket of his dark grey jacket and fished out a rectangle of paper. He then produced a pen from his waistcoat and, brushing aside a few crumbs on the paper, began to write. "There," he said and proceeded to feed the paper into his mouth.

"Alistair, you don't have to be so literal!"

His colleague continued to chew and made a big show of swallowing.

"For goodness sake, man, you'll choke."

"It's only rice paper," Alistair assured him at last with a grin. "Quite yummy, in fact. It contained a date bar."

Rex shook his head and smiled indulgently at his friend. Alistair was partial to nutritional snacks along with adolescent pranks. "Well, it certainly is strange that a judge's wig goes missing from one place and turns up in another. I shall tell Phoebe, but I'd like to speak to Richard first. I feel like I'm missing something."

Their food arrived and they concentrated on eating since they had to get back to Chambers Street for a one o'clock meeting with the Solicitor General, deputy to the Lord Advocate who headed the Crown Office and Procurator Fiscal Service. Piers Smiley was an affable man, well suited to his name, and Rex liked and respected him immensely.

In the middle of the afternoon he found time to ring Helen from his office and give her an update on his private case. "Looks like Phoebe's intuition, or whatever it was regarding her father, was true," he told her. "And I'm looking at Dan Sutter as being somehow involved."

"In that case, I feel contrite. It was uncharitable of me to dismiss her suspicions so lightly."

"I had my doubts too. As did Alistair. He went and ate his words. Wrote them down and chugged down the lot with some ale. It was only rice paper, but the silly sod had me going for a while."

Helen laughed. "That is so like him. So, is it back to Canterbury this weekend?" she asked, sounding disappointed.

"That would be the logical step. But I want to see Richard Pruitt again and perhaps one or two other people. Thaddeus, my friendly investigator in London, has been doing background checks on some ex-cons Judge Murgatroyd put away, and he said there was one in particular I should look at."

"A female?"

"Male. Originally from Kent. If I do go to Canterbury, how would you like to stay in a nice little hotel for the weekend and keep me company? That way I won't have to impose on Phoebe."

"I hardly think it would be imposing; I'm sure she'd just love to have you. No, I'd like to spend a weekend away with you, Rex, but only if I could have you all to myself. You'd only be distracted, and I don't see how I could be much use to you on this case. But perhaps you could stop by again?"

He said he would certainly try. He missed her; and her semi-detached home on Barley Close was a haven of peace and normality. Peaceful and normal could not in any way describe the day he was having as he attempted to pack in everything that needed to be done before he could make further plans for the weekend. This included tracking down the ex-felon Bruce Burke.

Through contacting his parole officer, Rex finally got hold of his suspect at the local auto shop where he worked. Thaddeus had sent a mugshot, which looked ominous to say the least, and Rex arranged to meet him in a very public place the next day.

TWENTY-SEVEN

A THUGGISH-LOOKING MAN WITH a shaved head, Bruce Burke did his arrest photo justice. A tattoo in poisonous green ink of a rattle-snake, poised to strike, coiled around his thick neck above the collar of his black sweatshirt.

"Thanks for meeting me," Rex said, surprised that Burke had agreed to give up part of his Friday afternoon at relative short notice.

The man's piercing grey eyes swept the teashop as he moved to-wards a corner table and selected a chair facing the entrance.

A woman in a full apron, with ginger hair pulled back in a sloppy ponytail, flicked a damp rag around the Formica table top. "Your usual, luv?" she asked Burke.

"No, just tea, ta." Burke spoke with a southern English accent and was missing two teeth from the bottom row.

"Same for me," Rex said.

She ambled away, greeting customers by name.

"You're not from here originally, are you?" Rex enquired.

"Kent."

"Been back there since your release?"

"Not yet. I have roots here now."

"You have a brother in Canterbury."

"I do," Burke said cautiously. "I thought you said on the phone this was about Dan Sutter."

"It is, but I heard that your brother Alan is the handyman of an acquaintance of mine, whose father sentenced Sutter to ten years in prison."

"Judge Murder sentenced me, and all. Al said he did odd jobs at his house and joked about doing something to make it look like the old geezer met with an accident. 'Course, he was only joking."

"Of course," Rex said, betraying no sarcasm.

"Al told me he died in his sleep."

"Are you glad he's dead?"

"I'd be lying if I said I wasn't."

"Do you keep in regular contact with your brother?"

Burke leaned back in his chair, his hands loosely clasped on the table. "We talk on the phone about once a month. He came to visit me in prison a couple of times, once with my niece. There's a ten-year age difference between me and Al, me being the youngest. Tim, our middle brother, died of a drug overdose. I was headed the same way before I was sent down for holding up a jeweller's. Daft, that was."

He clenched a giant fist stamped with gothic lettering across the knuckles, which Rex could not read. "There was cameras all over the shop, but I was high on ice and desperate for cash." His hand spread open in a gesture of resignation.

"Can you tell me how you got on with Dan Sutter? I understand you were cell mates."

"We had adjoining cells for a time. You try to get on with everyone inside, if you know what's good for you, but Dan wasn't what you'd call friendly. And he wasn't one to make confessions, not him. So, if that's what you wanted from me, you're out of luck. Sorry."

"What did he talk aboot?"

"His sister mostly. Said he should've been a better brother. Said what a monster his dad was. A lot of blokes inside talk about their girlfriends and wives. With him it was his sister. Whatever gets you through your stretch."

"Did he ever say he wanted to harm Judge Murgatroyd?"

"We all did. Everyone up before Judge Murder knew they were for it."

"Did he get into specifics?"

"Said how he'd like to carve him up in small pieces. I didn't pay much attention to the talk that went on inside, just did my time and got early release last year for good behaviour. And I won't be going back in neither. I got a decent paying job round the corner from this caffe, and me and the missus are going to have a baby. A bit late in life to start a family, you might be thinking, but I've a lot of time to make up for."

The waitress reappeared with the tea. Burke hunched forward and looped his hands around his mug protectively, no doubt a habit formed in prison.

"How old is the niece who came to visit you?" Rex asked.

"Petra? Twenty-two."

"What does she do?"

"Right now she's stocking shelves at Tesco's, but she's going to night school. Wants to do hair. Why're you interested in her?"

Rex took up the glass container of sugar and tipped the metal chute into his mug without comment.

TWENTY-EIGHT

THAT EVENING, REX SAT in Alistair's library in a purposefully distressed leather armchair in keeping with the floor-to-ceiling mahogany shelves and panelled wainscoting. At Alistair's prompting, he told him about his latest interview in the Murgatroyd case.

"I think Bruce Burke can be eliminated. He's a converted meth-head, who claims he's gone straight. Definitely not the rough individual I expected. He didn't seem to be harbouring any grudges and appeared to just want to get on with his life."

"So, crossed off the list?" Alistair squeezed a wedge of lemon into his Earl Grey.

"Aye, but he has a twenty-two-year-old niece living in Canterbury, who could conceivably have climbed into Judge Murgatroyd's room. That might explain the hair clasp found in the bed. Her dad is Phoebe's handyman, whom I told you aboot." Rex shrugged at the possibility of the niece's involvement, uncomfortable with how thin a possibility it was. Still, he was not ready to discount it quite yet.

"You're more convinced, now that the judge's wig turned up in Richard's flat, that it was Dan Sutter who broke into the house," Alistair stated, accustomed to his friend's way of presenting hypotheses only to dismiss them.

"I have no proof he was ever in England, but whether he broke into Phoebe's home or not, he still tried to kill Richard. For that alone I'd like him found."

"And he inflicted bodily harm on us," Alistair pointed out, sitting back in his brown leather wing armchair, his legs crossed at the ankles. "He had to find a way of getting rid of you before you realized he wasn't Richard Pruitt and alerted the police. When I came along, he probably couldn't believe his rotten luck, especially if Richard didn't receive many visitors. I'm sure Sutter was spying on him."

Rex thought for a moment as he contemplated his tumbler of whisky. "But I'm at a loss as to why he would tip his hand by leaving Judge Murgatroyd's wig in Richard Pruitt's attic."

"He has nothing to lose. He's already on the run. It could be either a message to Richard to desist in his private vendetta against him or one to you to stop assisting him. Or both."

"I thought he drugged and subdued me because I walked in on his disposal of Richard. How would he know of my interest in the Showers case? I could have been visiting Richard at his home for any number of reasons. When did you say he would be back?"

"Shortly. He went home with a police escort to retrieve his laptop and grab a change of clothes. It looks like he'll be staying until Dan Sutter is caught." Alistair cocked an ear. "I think that's him now." He went to the tall window. "Yes, the police car has just dropped him off."

"I'll go down," Rex said, getting up from the armchair.

"Tell him dinner will be ready in an hour, if he wants to join us. I'm making paella."

Rex descended the front stone steps to the pavement and continued down to the basement where he knocked on a black door fitted with brass fixtures. A few minutes passed before it opened.

"Sorry to keep you waiting," Richard said. "I had to check who it was. You never know, do you?" He stepped aside to let Rex into the hall.

"I've never been down here," Rex said, looking about him and sticking his head into the ultra-modernized eat-in kitchen. "Very nice."

The basement had been converted into a self-contained flat and redecorated to a high level of finish, just as Alistair had boasted.

"It's so kind of your friend to let me stay here." Richard led him into a sitting room furnished with plush modern furniture. "Please take a seat. Would you like a drink?"

Rex shook his head. "I just had one upstairs, thank you."

"Alistair made a lovely dinner last night. And I met John."

"You're invited tonight," Rex told him. "I'll be there. Not sure his partner will be."

"He said John was on nights. I wouldn't like to be an ambulance man. All those car accidents and crime scenes."

"Should I tell Alistair it's a yes?"

Richard nodded. "By all means. I brought food from my refrigerator at home so it doesn't go to waste, but I can eat it tomorrow."

Rex took the phone from his pocket and relayed the message to Alistair. He turned his attention back to Richard. "I meant to ask you if Sutter has a car. I'm hoping your PI saw the number plate."

"Sutter doesn't own a car. He always took the bus. My investigator said he was a slippery character."

"Well, he's managed to give police the slip." Rex then told him about his meeting with Stu Showers.

"So you do believe me?" Pruitt asked, beside himself with glee. "You must realize I had no motive to murder his daughter." He sighed and shook his bald head. "I would never have been associated with the Showers family had I not decided to go to a different pub that night. I'm a creature of habit, so why I deviated from my normal routine, I'll never know."

"One of the inexplicable vagaries of life," Rex remarked.

"Well, I rue that fateful decision to this day. No good deed goes unpunished," Pruitt announced querulously. "I went to the lass's rescue, not realizing she was dead, and it's hounded me since. I avoid dark and secluded places now, not because I don't want anything to happen to me; I just don't want to be in the position of stumbling upon something again and being falsely accused."

"And I would not have been involved in this matter had Phoebe Wells not asked for my help."

"You won't make your investigation public until you can prove Sutter killed April Showers, will you? I don't want my name dragged through the mud again."

Rex assured him he wouldn't.

"Good," said Pruitt, easing his posture in his chair.

"But I need proof. What was in the stolen shoebox?"

"Records of Sutter's comings and goings. Information concerning his background: how his father drank and beat him and his mother, and his teenage sister ran away. His mother left Edinburgh two years ago after her divorce."

"Where did she go?"

"I can't remember. But it's in the file."

Much good that did them, Rex thought a trifle irritably, and unfairly. After all, it wasn't Pruitt's fault the shoebox had been stolen. He had taken the precaution of hiding it, though to no avail as it turned out. Sutter must have searched the flat from top to bottom, leaving no sign he had done so, other than replacing the box with a wig on a papier-mâché bust.

"Do you remember the mother's name?" Rex asked Pruitt.

"Ann Sutter. His sister's name is Amber."

"And where did she go?"

"Amber? Wales, I think. Her mother might have joined her there after she divorced."

Rex received a call from Alistair to say dinner was ready, and the two men left the basement flat to go up to the main house.

"What would you like to listen to?" Alistair asked, standing by his Swedish stereo system.

"Oh, do play *La Traviata* again," Pruitt said. "The recording you have is so divine."

The dining room, separated by two arched pillars from the drawing room, was set for three, with a full array of china and silverware and peach-coloured napkins folded into fans in the wine goblets.

For all that Alistair had called Pruitt a bit cuckoo, they shared similar interests. Preoccupied with his own thoughts, Rex listened with scant attention while they discussed the latest fads in home improvement over the meal.

"Oh, I know!" Pruitt was agreeing with their host. "I got rid of all the brass in my flat. So *passé!*"

"Just wait five years and it'll be back in," was Rex's sole contribution to the topic.

Alistair told Pruitt about the American interior designer who had worked on Rex's retreat in the Highlands.

"Oh, a retreat," Pruitt exclaimed. "Where?"

"It's a converted hunting lodge near Gleneagle Village." Rex did not want to divulge too much about its location since it was, after all, a retreat, and he didn't want people dropping by unannounced.

"Do you spend much time there?"

"Not as much as my fiancée Helen and I would like."

"Oh, congratulations. I didn't know you were engaged. I hope I may meet the bride-to-be."

"McBride," Rex murmured.

"Oh, is that her surname?"

"I thought it was d'Arcy," Alistair interjected.

"It is," Rex said, impatient in his excitement. He addressed Pruitt. "You said Dan Sutter's mother was called Ann Sutter. I wonder if McBride is her maiden name. If so, she goes by Annie now."

"Possibly," Pruitt said in confusion. "She may well have changed her name back when she divorced her drunk of a husband. But I don't know of a McBride."

Annie had told Phoebe she was a widow, as Rex recalled. "Are you sure she moved to Wales?"

"Her daughter went to Wales, but now that I think on it, the mother moved to England."

"Could she have gone to Kent?"

"Perhaps. Or Essex. One of the home counties, at any rate. Is Essex a home county?"

Alistair affirmed that it was, since it bordered on London.

"According to my PI's report, she works as a home help or something of the kind."

"Does Canterbury ring a bell?" Rex asked hopefully.

"Could be Canterbury. Or Colchester. That's in Essex, isn't it?" Pruitt asked, looking first at Rex and then at Alistair, who nodded and added that Colchester was the oldest Roman town in Britain.

"She couldn't be Phoebe Wells' housekeeper, by any chance?" Rex persisted.

"I very much doubt it," Pruitt answered. "The judge would have mentioned to me if Sutter's mother was employed by his daughter."

"If he'd known. Two years ago is when you said she left Edinburgh. And, lo and behold, Annie has been in Phoebe Wells' employ for two years. Did you ever tell Judge Murgatroyd you suspected Sutter was April Showers' killer?"

"Well, naturally. I hoped he could pull a few strings, but he didn't seem inclined to discuss matters of law. To be honest, I'm not sure he wasn't going a bit gaga in his old age."

Rex ruminated for a few moments as he scooped up the last of his paella. He sat back in his chair, thought for a moment more, and suddenly announced he had to leave.

"Are you not staying for dessert?" Alistair asked. "I have a sublime zabaglione from—"

"Next time," Rex said, getting up from the table to a mounting crescendo of soprano from the stereo system.

He thanked his friend for dinner and told Pruitt he would be in touch the next day. He had to make an urgent call.

TWENTY-NINE

REX'S THOUGHTS RACED IN all directions as he drove home to Morningside. Ann Sutter living and working under Phoebe's roof ... Was it possible? If so, Dan Sutter might have known Pruitt was in contact with the judge who had deprived him of ten years of freedom. The placing of the wig in Pruitt's flat now made more sense.

The attempt on Pruitt's life could be about more than Pruitt tailing him. Sutter had wanted to stop Pruitt blabbing about his involvement in the Showers murder. And he would know about Rex's investigation if Annie had been listening in on his conversations with Phoebe. It was all beginning to come together at last, but he had to be certain.

Only when he got to his bedroom and saw the luminous green hands on the alarm clock did he realize the time. He debated ringing Phoebe or waiting until morning. Then he saw that she had called him earlier without leaving a message. He decided that what he had to tell her was important enough to wake her if she was in bed.

She answered almost immediately, and he apologized for the late hour.

"I was only watching TV," she assured him. "You're a welcome distraction."

"Well, I'm not sure how welcome this will be, but it may prove distracting. Can anyone hear you?"

"Why? What is it?" Phoebe asked in alarm. "Do you have news?"

"I may. Can you call me back on a mobile?"

"I will if it's charged."

Rex waited a few minutes before he heard his phone ring. On the display he saw an unfamiliar number with the Canterbury area code.

"It's me," she said in a low voice. "I'm in my bedroom on my mobile. I hate these stupid things."

He told her what he had learned from Pruitt. "Is there any chance Dan Sutter could be your housekeeper's son?" he asked.

"Annie's? She's never mentioned a son! Wait while I close the door," Phoebe said in a hushed tone. "Are you sure?"

"No, but I thought I should warn you of the possibility."

"If that's the case," Phoebe resumed quietly so Rex had to strain to hear, "my father must not have recognized her from court, if she attended her son's trial, which I assume she did. But his eyesight was failing, as was his memory, and the trial was a long time ago. Plus, he wasn't exactly chatty, as you know, so he wouldn't have asked her about her private life. For another thing, he was of the generation not to treat domestics as equals. Doug used to chide him about it." She paused. "Do you really think Annie would purposely seek employment in this house to avenge her son's incarceration?"

Rex did not answer immediately. It had not occurred to him that Annie might be responsible for more than perhaps leaving the window unlocked. "How did she know you were seeking a home help?"

"I advertised in *The Lady*."

"You said she had the evening off the night your father passed," he probed.

"Yes. She went to the cinema and stayed over at a friend's."

"What time did she leave the house?"

"Around five."

"And what time did you say you checked in on your father?"

"When I went up to bed. I'm sure he was still alive at that point."

"You mentioned that he had Horlicks at bedtime. Who prepared that?"

"I did that night. At around nine."

"You made it in the kitchen?"

"There's nowhere else in the house to prepare it. What are you suggesting, Rex?" Phoebe asked in a worried voice.

"I don't know yet. I still need confirmation that your housekeeper is Dan Sutter's mother."

"Well," Phoebe faltered, "you've met her. She's reserved and a bit dour, but I couldn't stand to have one of those cheerful women nattering on all day long, and Dad had no patience for idle chitterchatter. Oh, my goodness," she exclaimed under her breath. "Do you think it's safe here?" Rex heard her bolt the bedroom door. "I doubt I'll get much sleep tonight," she told him in weary resignation, to which he apologized. "Should I ask Annie to leave immediately, saying I don't really need her now that Dad is gone?"

Rex couldn't reliably answer the question of her safety. "Only if you can do so without arousing suspicion," he advised. Perhaps Phoebe should be more concerned about the son. Was he still in Scotland, or was he in Essex with his sister? Did Annie even have a daughter and grandchildren in Brightlingsea? Pruitt thought her daughter had gone to live in Wales.

"Are you sure she's not eavesdropping?" he asked.

"She went to bed hours ago. I went to the kitchen earlier for a snack, and the TV was off. I didn't hear a peep from her room. Anyway, Annie is an elderly woman. What could she do to me? All the same, I'm going to push my dressing table in front of the door. My window faces the street. There's no easy way for someone to climb up. This is Annie's weekend off and she usually takes off early on Saturday morning."

"I almost forgot. You rang while I was having dinner with Alistair and Richard. Was it important?"

"Oh, it was about the stamp album. I showed it to an expert in Knightsbridge. He pretty much agreed with what Christopher Penn told you. So, unless there was something really valuable in the unfinished album ... But if there were, I don't think Dad would have left it out on the desk."

Rex noticed the clock hands approaching eleven o'clock. He told Phoebe he would try to make it to Canterbury on Sunday. She sounded relieved, and he could only imagine what sort of night she would spend, processing the new information and all its implications.

THIRTY

THE NEXT MORNING REX got up early and called Richard Pruitt from the breakfast table.

"Is your PI talking to the police?" he asked Pruitt.

"No, Adrian Glover doesn't work with the police," Pruitt said sleepily, and Rex suspected he had woken him up.

"And why not?"

"He used to be one of them, but he got kicked off the force."

"How come?"

"He was on the take. He said he wasn't, though. The point is, he knows how they work, which is useful, and he's cheap."

Rex was not surprised, what with those credentials. "Do you mind if I meet with him?"

"Not at all, but not here. I don't want him leading Sutter to Albany Street, especially as Alistair has been so gracious as to allow me to stay. Do you want his number?"

Rex wasted no time ringing Glover, who was reluctant to meet, until Rex persuaded him he would make it worth his while. After having to wait until the private investigator called Pruitt for authorization to speak to him, he and Glover set up a time and place. Rex hurried to the appointment by George IV Bridge near the life-size statue of Greyfriars Bobby, the nineteenth-century Skye Terrier that had watched over his master's grave for fourteen long years.

"Thank you for meeting me so early," Rex addressed the slight figure in a belted poplin raincoat huddled on the bench where they had arranged to speak.

"I don't sleep much." Glover had boot-polish black hair combed back with gel and he wore glasses with square frames. A more conspicuous sleuth was hard to imagine in Rex's opinion.

Gusts of wind whirled litter about their feet and ruffled the feathers of sparrows hopping about in search of crumbs. The PI looked ahead without making eye contact while answering Rex's questions hurriedly and furtively. Rex felt as though he were receiving classified trade secrets instead of information about the life and habits of Daniel T. Sutter. He asked specifically if the ex-con had ever left Edinburgh prior to his disappearance.

"Some weeks ago he started making trips to London by train. Purchased tickets, once to Victoria and once to Paddington Station. Beyond there, I don't know. It wasn't within my budget to follow him further afield than Edinburgh. My client terminated my services before I could write up the report, and just when things starting to get interesting."

"Do you have those dates for me?"

"I do."

"And did you bring the phone number I asked for?"

"I did. And remuneration for my trouble?"

Rex slipped him a fifty-pound note, hoping it would end up being money well spent. Glover passed him the telephone number scribbled on the back of a business card headed "A. Glover & Co. Private Investigations. Discretion Assured."

He then dug into a pocket of his beige raincoat and produced a small diary bound in dark patent leather, which he opened and perused, flipping through the entries. He extracted two pages and handed them to Rex, who thanked him.

"You have no idea, Mr. Graves, how much of my profession consists of just watching and waiting," said the PI, staring straight ahead of him.

"Not sure I'd have the patience," Rex remarked, although he considered he had more than most. "Did he ever catch you following him?"

Glover's rail-thin body stiffened on the bench. "Never," he said with indignation. "I know that's what my client thinks, but no. Dan Sutter did go to considerable lengths to cover his tracks, doubling back on buses and darting into alleyways, but I am relentless, Mr. Graves. Relentless. I stuck to him like an invisible shadow all the time he was in Edinburgh."

As light raindrops began to fall on Rex's bare head, the investigator pulled a cloche hat from his pocket and covered his uniformly black hair.

Bidding him goodbye, Rex got up from the bench and headed back to Morningside. He popped open his brolly. The drizzle made the steep-stepped roofs and quiet Saturday morning streets all the more grey, and the few people he passed seemed not at all happy to be out and about so early.

He thought Glover a funny wee man and perhaps not altogether trustworthy. The PI had supplied the number of Amber Sutter, now Mason, who lived near Cardiff in Wales in an unpronounceable town or village full of the letters *d*, *l*, and *y*, but Rex questioned whether it was valid information. Consequently, he was somewhat surprised when half an hour later a woman with an eroded but discernible Scots accent answered his call.

"How did you find me?" she demanded when he addressed her by her maiden name.

"I'm an advocate depute at the High Court in Edinburgh. I'm helping someone in a case that might involve your brother."

"I can't help you. I've had nothing to do with my family in thirty years."

"I understand you ran away from home when you were a young girl."

"I don't want to talk about it. Neither my mother nor brother lifted a finger to protect me from my father, and they can go hang now." The phone went dead in Rex's ear.

If what she had suffered was true, Rex was glad she had left her past behind her. He was the last person to divulge her whereabouts and would have told her as much if she had given him the chance.

At least he knew for sure she was in Wales and not in Brightlingsea, where her mother said she visited her and her granddaughters. Glover had confirmed Ann Sutter's maiden name and the fact there was no other daughter. Annie McBride had been caught in a lie. And where there was one, more were sure to follow.

Next he called Phoebe. "I can come to Canterbury tomorrow," he told her, "on my way to Brightlingsea to search for Dan Sutter. You said it was a small town."

"Yes, unless it's grown significantly since I was last there. But what makes you think he's in Brightlingsea?"

"The police have been searching for him in Edinburgh and in northwest Scotland with no success. Brightlingsea seems as likely a place as any for him to be staying, since his mother makes frequent trips there."

"To see her daughter."

"Whom Pruitt's private investigator tracked to Wales," Rex informed Phoebe. "I just spoke to her and she was not pleased to be found. She wants nothing to do with her family. The point is, she's not in Brightlingsea, and she's Annie's only daughter. There's a lot to explain. I can be there around lunchtime tomorrow, if that suits you? May I bring someone?"

"Your fiancée?"

"My colleague Alistair. If I'm going to look in Brightlingsea, I'll need a car and someone to help me, so we'll be driving down. Alistair is already involved in the case."

"It could be dangerous!" Phoebe lowered her voice, which had been rising in hysteria. "Sutter tried to kill Richard Pruitt, for goodness' sake. He might attack you."

"Alistair managed to fend him off last time."

Phoebe sighed. "Well, by all means bring your friend, and stay as long as you need to. He's more than welcome and I'd love to meet him. I just don't like the idea of you going after Dan Sutter. Did you tell the detectives on the case you were going to Brightlingsea?"

"I'll call them when I'm on the road. I'm leaving very soon, but stopping overnight in Derby to see Helen and break up the journey."

Phoebe made an "oh" sound and wished him a safe trip.

THIRTY-ONE

AT NOON, ALISTAIR COLLECTED Rex from his house in his silver Jaguar, which was far more comfortable than his colleague's compact Mini Cooper.

"Road trip!" Alistair crowed from the rolled down car window. He seemed to have warmed to the idea of going after Sutter since Rex had rung him that morning.

"A long run will do her good." He tapped the outside of the shiny driver's-side door.

"Did you pack casual clothes?" Rex asked, placing his bag on the leather back seat, where Alistair's Burberry coat lay neatly folded. This was his colleague's idea of casual, apparently.

"You told me to and I did. And a weapon."

"Like what? Your fencing sword?" Rex buckled his seat belt as Alistair put the car in first gear and drove away from the curb.

"You may well laugh, but we all know what a nasty character Sutter is. I borrowed John's rubber baton to conk him on the head if need be. Some of the mentally ill patients John has to treat can get a bit combative. I would have brought a gun if I could get hold of one, but I've never even fired one."

"We'll bring the police in if we manage to get him cornered. Thank you for doing this, Alistair. I know it's short notice, but I had to get my ducks in a row first."

"Think nothing of it. I wouldn't want to miss out on a chance to pay Sutter back. And if I stayed at home, I'd only have to babysit Richard. John can keep a loose eye on him. He is a little bit needy is our friend Richard."

"Well, if we do catch Sutter, he'll be able to go home. But I can't promise anything. I'm mainly going on a hunch."

"Based on some pertinent facts," Alistair qualified. "That's good enough for me.

"I still find it odd that Sutter would have taken Judge Murg-atroyd's wig if he murdered him."

"I imagine he took it as a trophy. Possibly he took things of neg-ligible value so Phoebe would be less likely to notice or, if she did, less inclined to go to the police."

Rex rubbed his face in his hands and groaned. It was a lot to sort out, but if they could understand Sutter's motives, they might be able to anticipate his next move.

"Where are we staying tonight?" Alistair asked.

"At Helen's house in Derby. She's expecting us. And then on to Phoebe's."

"A woman in every port, eh?" Alistair joked as they left Morning-side behind and headed towards the A1.

"It's only two hours from Canterbury to Brightlingsea," Rex said, ignoring the comment. "I consulted a map."

"My satnav will give us all the directions we need." Alistair's dashboard had as many dials and displays as a commercial jet.

"I still prefer to rely on old-fashioned maps," Rex argued.

"Well, we can use both methods, old fruit."

Rex pulled his phone from his jacket pocket and called Helen to let her know that he and Alistair were setting out and when to expect them. She sounded excited at the prospect of seeing them later. He told her not to go to any trouble for dinner. They could go to Poppadoms. He assured her Alistair liked Indian food. Alistair nodded enthusiastically.

He then called Phoebe to say he and Alistair would be arriving in Canterbury the next day as planned. She sounded equally excited. After the calls, Rex nestled his head against the headrest and expelled a relieved sigh at having completed the arrangements.

"Yes, it must be tiring having two women on the go," Alistair said to rile him.

Rex told him in good humour to shut up and just drive. A classical music CD and an audio book later, interrupted midway by a stop for petrol, they arrived in Derby.

Rex gave directions to Barley Close, which he could find in his sleep, and Alistair compared them to those given by the automated navigator. Both sets of directions matched street for street and turning for turning, Rex keeping slightly ahead of the programmed male voice and declaring victory as they turned into Helen's driveway. She bounded out of the front door and threw herself into his waiting arms, her cornflower blue eyes sparkling up at him as she chatted with animation.

Next she gave Alistair a big hug. "So lovely to see you again. You made good time in your speed machine. And I just love how it looks in my driveway! Did you at least manage to get some lunch?"

"Stewed coffee and limp sandwiches at a service station. We're ready for a proper meal and a comfortable bed." Alistair stretched his long limbs as though to get rid of the kinks and proceeded to open the boot. "We'll be leaving at the crack of dawn," he added with a wry grin.

"I only have a single bed in the guest room," Helen apologized. "I think it's only six feet and you're almost as tall as Rex."

"Don't worry," Alistair assured her. "I was a student once."

"At some posh Oxford college," Rex interjected, winking at Helen before reaching into the back seat for his own bag.

"I made a quiche, which I'll pack for your breakfast with a Thermos of coffee, so you can eat on the road to save time."

"No need for you to get up early, lass."

"I want to see you off. I insist."

Once Helen made up her mind, there was little point in arguing, and Rex merely squeezed her with his free arm. The three of them made their way down the path to the front door of her semi-detached home, which greeted Rex with its familiar scent of vanilla from the candles she liked to burn in the evening.

Over and above the joy he felt to be back with Helen, he felt a thrill of excitement. He was half way closer geographically to finding his quarry.

"You will be careful," Helen murmured in the narrow hallway, nestling her head against his shoulder.

"Oh, aye," he assured her, kissing her blonde hair. "And don't forget I have Alistair to protect me."

"If I don't die of hunger first."

"Well, let's get you both fed. We can leave as soon as you're ready."

Dinner at the Indian restaurant proved a joyful affair, Alistair being in fine form and mimicking some characters of his and Rex's acquaintance. Helen laughed until the tears streamed down her face. Not to be outdone, Rex gave a humorous account of his meeting with Pruitt's PI, whom he described as an inept master of disguise and felt sure kept a false moustache in the pocket of his raincoat.

As if by tacit agreement, little reference was made to the men's imminent, semi-clandestine excursion as they tucked into their banquet of Tandoori chicken, Madras curry, and naan bread served on a gold-embroidered tablecloth beneath the glass table top.

However, after Alistair had gone to bed, Helen asked about the case, and it began to consume Rex's thoughts, even in sleep. At one point, Judge Murgatroyd appeared as a red-bodied spider at the core of a wide black web, its threads extending in all directions. Rex awoke with a start.

He settled back into the pillows, unwilling to relinquish the vestiges of the dream, in the hope of dissecting its meaning. No doubt it held none, his subconscious merely trying to process a surfeit of information. And yet the mystery had begun with Judge Murgatroyd, and everyone Rex had interviewed in the course of his inquiry was caught in the web.

THIRTY-TWO

AN HOUR'S DRIVE FROM Canterbury, Rex and Alistair heard on the car radio that a new witness had come forward in the Lindsay Poulson case. This was the first mention in the media of the missing girl in a week, the trail having gone cold since that first day.

Alistair turned up the volume. The man substantiated the first eye witness account of a beige-striped brown van trolling near her school the afternoon she went missing. He had gone to Brussels on business the next day and had only seen the police poster when he returned.

"She's probably dead," Alistair said glumly when the news switched to an unrelated topic. "Statistically, it's unlikely she was kept alive for more than twenty-four hours, and it's been over a fortnight."

"That was the case with April Showers," Rex concurred. "She was murdered within six hours."

If Kent Police had not managed to trace a van described by two witnesses, what hope did the authorities have of finding the predator? He could be in Europe by now.

When Alistair pulled up in front of Phoebe's house on St. Dunstan's Terrace forty minutes later, Rex's backside was sore, in spite of the comfortable seating. He got out of the Jaguar with an immense sense of relief.

Before he had a chance to retrieve his bag, Phoebe came through the door and down the steps and welcomed them warmly. She held out her hand to Alistair, and he drew her into an embrace.

"So terribly sorry for all you've been through," he said with sincerity. Alistair could be frivolous at times, but he was also one of the most empathetic people Rex knew, along with Helen. He always had the right words to say and an appropriate gesture.

Phoebe looked touched. "Thank you, Alistair. Yes, it's been a difficult time since Dad's death. I don't know what I would have done without Rex."

She took Rex's arm. "He's very dashing," she whispered. "Shame he's the other way inclined. So, what's the plan?" she enquired in a normal voice when they reached the hallway.

"We're playing it a bit by ear," Rex replied.

"I've prepared a buffet lunch in the dining room. I'll show you to your rooms so you can freshen up, and then we can talk." Phoebe led them upstairs and showed Alistair into a guest bedroom on her floor while Rex went on up to the one he had been staying in on his two previous visits.

They reconvened in the dining room shortly afterwards and helped themselves to the selection of cold meats and cheeses set out on the sideboard. A basket of bread rolls and a tin of crackers waited on the table, along with a chilled bottle of white wine and a pot of coffee. Rex opted for the caffeine while Alistair joined Phoebe in a glass of Bordeaux.

"Now then," Phoebe said from the head of the table when they were all three installed with their lunch. "I'm thrilled you both could come. I've been rather anxious since Rex called me on Friday night."

"I take it your housekeeper left for Essex yesterday morning?" he asked.

"Yes, it's just us for the moment."

"Does she have a car?"

"She doesn't drive. I expect she took the train. She was gone by the time I got up."

"Did you end up barricading yourself in your room?" Rex asked with a smile.

"I did." Phoebe smiled apologetically at Alistair. "I'm afraid of a sixty-four-year-old woman!"

"Quite understandable under the circumstances," Alistair said in a reassuring tone while he buttered a roll.

"I'm worried now she might poison my food. But don't worry; I went shopping for our lunch this morning."

"I'm sorry it can't be more of a social visit," Rex said, "but Alistair and I planned on driving to Brightlingsea this afternoon."

"I quite understand. That's what you're here for, after all. The sooner we can get the business of the break-in and Dad's murder resolved, the better. I can't begin to tell you how grateful I am that you've taken my fears seriously."

Rex refrained from telling her about the judge's wig found in Pruitt's attic until he could be sure it belonged to her father. He looked across at Alistair, who was obviously content to eat and let him direct the conversation.

"According to Richard Pruitt's private investigator, Sutter took a train from Edinburgh to Victoria Station four days before your father's death. Of course, he could have gone anywhere from London, but the

160

timing is significant. Were you aware that Richard discussed his investigation of Dan Sutter with your father?" Rex asked. "That would be an additional motive for murder beyond being sentenced by him; if indeed we're on the right track and Sutter committed the crime."

"He gave updates, but Dad wasn't interested in getting involved in reopening the case. He just wanted to enjoy his retirement as best he could."

Rex wondered how much the housekeeper had heard of the judge's conversations. If he was a bit deaf, he possibly spoke loudly on the phone. And Annie could have listened in on an extension, which was why Rex had taken to talking to Phoebe on her mobile.

"There is a landline phone in the kitchen, correct? It's just that I never noticed one."

"There's one on every floor. Dad had one in his room. He didn't have a mobile."

"Does Annie?"

"I've never seen her use one."

If she was in regular touch with her son, she probably had an untraceable prepaid phone. Rex could only speculate how much she knew about his activities. Had she been sending him money now that he was off unemployment benefits? He had not been receiving any since his attack on Richard Pruitt at Ramsay Garden, according to Glover.

"You're sure her son murdered Dad?" Phoebe questioned him. "What about the pink hair clasp?"

"Annie may have planted it to mislead us and make us think it was a woman and not her son who broke in. Have you heard back from Constable Bryant?"

"Yes, he said there were no fingerprints on the clasp or piece of latex. A technician had examined them as a special favour for us."

Phoebe saw her other guest had finished eating and asked if he wanted a second helping.

"I had someone look into female offenders sentenced by your father," Rex said while Alistair got up to refill his plate. "No one of quite the right age came up." He helped himself to more coffee. "However, I discovered your handyman has a brother who was given a long stretch by your father, and he has a daughter of twenty-two."

"Alan Burke never mentioned a brother. Mind you, I'm not sure I'd want to talk about a brother in prison. What did he do?"

"Robbed a jeweller's at gunpoint."

"Goodness. That is a strange coincidence, isn't it? Dad having sent Alan's brother down, I mean. But the idea of his daughter breaking into the house ... I don't know about that," Phoebe said in a hesitant voice. "I saw her once when she dropped him off in his van. Rather a dumpy girl, not the sort you could imagine climbing a drainpipe!"

"The list of male suspects, on the other hand, is as long as my arm, including the brother. But Bruce Burke managed to persuade me, for the moment at least, that he has not been back to Kent since his release. For now I'm pursuing Dan Sutter as our most likely suspect and Annie as an accomplice."

"Her involvement makes me very uncomfortable." Phoebe looked temporarily dazed.

"She may have no knowledge," Rex conceded. "But in view of the fact she took the position at your house ... "

"Premeditation," Alistair said, returning to the table with a full plate. "I daresay she supplied fictitious references."

Rex was glad to see him pour himself a cup of coffee. It could turn into a long day, and they had been up since dawn.

"She's due back tonight," Phoebe said. "What should I do?"

"We may find her before then," Alistair said optimistically.

"If not, try and act as normal as possible," Rex cautioned. "We should be back before you go to bed."

A shawl was draped over the back of Phoebe's chair. She wrapped herself in it even though the dining room was comfortably warm. Rex concentrated on eating while Alistair enquired about her "delightful" house, which he guessed correctly dated back to the late Regency period. He told her about his Georgian residence in Edinburgh's New Town. Phoebe visibly relaxed as they chatted, and Rex regretted having to interrupt.

"The sooner we get going, the sooner we can get back," he said. "That was a grand lunch, Phoebe."

"Oh, don't you want some rhubarb pie? Annie made it."

"I don't think so, thank you," Alistair demurred. "I've already eaten far too much."

Rex could not be sure whether his friend was suspicious of Annie's pie or was simply watching his waistline, but he politely declined as well.

"Perhaps we could take some fruit with us," Alistair asked.

"Of course." Phoebe went to the sideboard and pulled a large napkin from a drawer, which she used to bundle up some bananas and apples. "I hope the police know you're going to Brightlingsea to look for Dan Sutter."

"DCI Lauper didn't seem very interested," Rex replied. "Probably didn't want to go on another fool's errand after a false sighting on the island of Lewis. He said we were to call his counterpart in Colchester if we ran into trouble."

"Which we hopefully shall," Alistair said lightly. "That really is the whole point of our going, after all."

This elicited a small smile from Phoebe. "Well, be careful, both of you. I'll be on tenterhooks until you get back."

Rex promised to ring and give her a progress report once they had a better idea of the situation. He and Alistair gathered what they needed in their search for Dan Sutter and set out for Essex without further delay.

THIRTY-THREE

Heading out of Canterbury towards the Dartford Tunnel and proceeding northeast on the A12, Rex and Alistair encountered little Sunday traffic.

Rex's impression of Essex, as the Jaguar ate up the miles of carriageway bypassing several towns on the way to Colchester, was that it was flat and un-scenic and rendered all the less prepossessing that afternoon by an overcast sky.

The rest of the journey proved uneventful as he and Alistair discussed their immediate plans and entertained various scenarios; and less than two hours after leaving Phoebe's house, they were entering Brightlingsea from Thorrington Cross on the B1029.

The road curved past an old parish church on a hill and continued past a school to their left and the Cherry Tree Pub on their right. They came to Victoria Place, the location of several banks and businesses, and took a random turn into a narrow street with cars parked alongside the two-storey, semi-detached homes in red brick standing flush on the pavement. Some had been whitewashed or otherwise given a face-lift. Others presented rough rendered façades, a few retaining their original sash windows. The overall impression was dreary in the late afternoon.

The street made a slight kink in its route leading to the waterfront. The two men stepped out of the car to the screeching of gulls wheeling in a watery blue sky. A tang of seaweed assailed Rex's nose as he watched the greenish grey water crested with dingy foam slosh against the concrete seawall.

Set back from the promenade, a semi-circle of wooden beach huts painted in bright shades or pastels stretched around the promontory, which he guessed from the topography had originally been marshland.

A handful of dinghies skimmed across the broad river beyond that joined the sea, tacking at cross angles with tautly stretched sails. The wind was picking up and throwing Alistair's hair into uncharacteristic disarray and stinging Rex's eyes.

"Now that we've got our bearings, let's start on the pubs," he suggested, heading back to the car. "I'm ready for a pint and even more eager to find Dan Sutter."

Pruitt's investigator had said he frequented pubs. If Annie's daughter was not here, the ex-Mrs. Sutter would have come for the purpose of visiting her son, Rex kept convincing himself. But where were they staying? If the pubs did not pan out, he and Alistair would have to start over again with the hotels, hostels, and rental accommodations, asking for guests and tenants by the name of McBride. It was almost certain neither would use the name Sutter. Adding to the daunting prospect was the inconvenience of it being a Sunday, when tourist and rental offices might be closed.

"A pub crawl with a purpose," Alistair said, starting the throaty car engine. "How many pubs did you say?"

"At least six. We'll start at the Rosebud and work our way back."

The only downside to the Jaguar was that it was conspicuous. The trip from Edinburgh had muted some of its silvery gleam, and flying insects had found their final resting place on the smeared windscreen, but the car's elongated lines drew many a glance as they drove to the first pub on Rex's list.

The Rosebud did not turn up anyone who had seen Sutter. Nor did the second pub. Admittedly, the photo from the police flyer was grainy.

Each equipped with a copy, Rex and Alistair then made the rounds of the Brewer's Arms, enquiring of every customer and member of staff whether they had seen the man in the picture. A local resident said he looked familiar, before realizing it was because his ex-brother-in-law had the same sort of bland face, although it couldn't be him because he had died in a motorcycle accident two years ago.

"He's a criminal, right?" another customer asked, studying Sutter's face. "It's in the eyes if you look closely enough. Is he wanted for something?" Rex had removed the "wanted" part of the flyer before showing it around.

"Attempting to murder a man in Edinburgh," Rex vaguely divulged. He requested that he not say anything to anyone until the subject of their search had been found. The customer, by all appearances a reasonable sort enjoying a pint before he went home to dinner, obligingly agreed.

"What's left?" Alistair asked when they were back on the street in the damp grey evening, the air heavy with the promise of rain.

Rex consulted the list. "Let's try the Masthead, down by the water."

"I'm assuming this used to be a fishing village," Alistair remarked on the drive to the pub.

"From what I've read, Brightlingsea used to have an oyster industry. And shipbuilding. It's situated at the mouth of a tidal river. I imagine it's a dormitory town for Colchester now, judging by the number of newer homes back there." By newer, Rex meant post-war.

They parked near the centre of town and continued by foot. The co-op they passed was closed, or Rex would have asked inside about Dan Sutter. Presumably he had to shop somewhere if he was in town.

Rex did not want to admit to Alistair that he was beginning to lose hope, especially when his friend remained ebulliently positive. Brightlingsea was bigger than he had thought it would be. And yet only that morning he had felt deep in his bones that it was the place to look. He put his discouragement down to the two days of travel following a busy week. After all, they had barely begun looking.

The Masthead appeared more rundown than the other pubs. The windows within the weathered frames were so encrusted with salt and grime that Rex was unable to see clearly into the gloomy interior.

They went in and ordered drinks as they casually glanced around at the patrons, many of them engrossed in a rowdy game of darts taking place at the far end of the bar by an empty, charred fireplace. Rex showed the barman the photo, expecting the usual response.

He nodded and said, "He comes in here from time to time. What's he done?"

"What makes you say that?"

The barman skewed his jaw. "Can't say exactly, but somefing's a bit off about him, know what I mean?"

"He came into some money and we were assigned the task of finding him." Alistair made it sound like an unenviable chore.

"Did he win the pools?"

"No," Alistair replied. "He was left it by a distant relative. We represent the estate."

Rex knew they had to find Sutter before someone told him they were searching for him. He came from a family without money and would be highly suspicious if he heard the flimsy story they had concocted. However, greed was a great motivator and the barman already had pound signs in his eyes.

"He's a mate of mine is Danny Boy. You tell him to say hello to Ray at the Masthead when you find him. Hasn't been round here since Thursday night, I think it was."

An old man in a flat cap sitting on a barstool raised his tankard of beer to the two men as they took up their drinks. Rex cheerfully returned the gesture. They finally had proof Sutter was in Brightlingsea, or had been here recently!

Rex turned back to the barman, whose hair was thinning at the temples, age lines grooved into his face, and tried to gauge how far he could be trusted. "If you could maybe point us in the right direction, you'd be doing Danny a service, and us. It's been a long day. As soon as we can have him sign the letter informing him of his inheritance, we can be on our way."

"Is it much, you know, of an inheritance?" Ray asked, leaning forward and placing his bare forearms upon the sticky bar.

Rex smiled conspiratorially. "We're not really at liberty to say, but I'd consider it a windfall if I were the lucky recipient."

"It'd be one for him an' all, judging by his clothes. I can't swear to it, but I think he's staying at the campsite out yonder." Ray pointed through the impenetrable window.

"Who's that then?" asked a beer-bellied customer approaching the bar from the direction of the dartboard.

"That bloke Danny what drinks McEwan's was in here Thursday."

"I seen him earlier in the week at the campsite. I'm always over there fixing the drains. What about him?"

"These gentlemen come from … Where'd you say you come from again?" the barman asked.

"London," Alistair replied.

"Just wondered 'cos your colleague sounds like he's Scottish, same as Danny."

"Originally from Edinburgh."

"That's where he's from an' all."

Definitely our man, Rex congratulated himself. "Any idea what he drives?"

Ray shook his head. "No idea. What about you, Ken?"

The globular eyes in the plumber's shiny red face took on a vacant stare. "Can't say that I do, but you won't find many cars at the campsite now the season's over."

Rex chugged on his beer. "Well, best get on," he said to Alistair, settling their bill and adding a generous tip. "Good evening to you," he addressed Ray, Ken, and the old man on the barstool.

Leaving their half-finished drinks on the counter, they promptly exited the pub. Rex could feel the weight of the men's stares on his back. He turned up his coat collar, ostensibly against the sharp wind. "Let's get a move on before they decide to follow us to the campsite to see how Danny Boy receives the happy news."

"Sounds like he might not still be there from what they were saying. What's the plan?"

"We'll take the car as close as we can without being seen, in case we have to make a quick getaway."

"What if we actually find him? I'm sure he's never parted from his trusty knife."

"Once we find some evidence he's there, we'll call in the police and wait close by to make sure he does not escape."

"Escape again, you mean," said Alistair in a rare grim mood.

THIRTY-FOUR

The Colneside Touring and Caravan Site was empty, save for a few isolated motorhomes and caravans.

A handful of hardened tourists had pitched tents by a boating lake inhabited by ducks and swans gliding among the reeds. The only buildings on site consisted of a concrete block of showers and washrooms and a modest house, which Rex surmised must belong to the owner or manager. The blinds were drawn over dark windows and there was no sign of life.

"Look over there," Alistair called out softly in the failing light, pointing to a white commercial van parked by a motorhome gleaming black on the outer perimeter of the campground. "A second generation Iveco Daily," he said in a strained voice. Alistair was an expert on vehicles of all descriptions.

"If you're thinking what I think you're thinking, it's the wrong colour."

"We'll see. Come on."

They crossed the grassy terrain that ran to mud in places and approached the motorhome cautiously, in case someone was home. No light appeared within and no sound came from the generator outside.

Rex expelled his breath, which he realized he had been holding. They turned their attention back to the van.

"Looks like a recent spray job," Alistair observed by the faint glow of a lamppost. "Let's see what's underneath." He produced a penknife from his Burberry trench coat and, bending down, scraped at the white paint by the front wheel-well furthest away from the motorhome. "Look here…"

Rex crouched beside his colleague. "Brown paint?" he asked peering at the exposed spot. He took a slim electric torch from his coat pocket and shone its beam at the darker colour.

"And did you notice the dodgy number plate? The third and fourth digits indicate a much newer vehicle than this."

Rex glanced at Alistair, who stared back at him with as serious a face as he had ever seen on his friend.

"It's not all that far from Dover," Alistair said. "This might well be the van used in that schoolgirl's abduction. Could Dan Sutter have something to do with it?"

"Who knows?" Rex murmured grimly.

Lindsay Poulson had gone missing walking home from school, just as April Showers had. However, the two abductions were a decade apart and separated by the length of England and half of Scotland, and there was as yet insufficient proof that Sutter had been responsible for April's murder. However, it had become probable that he had been to Canterbury, and likely he was in Brightlingsea.

"Perhaps we'll know soon enough."

"Slash the tyre?" Alistair suggested.

"Good idea. If it's the van the police are looking for, we don't want it disappearing again."

Alistair punctured the worn tyre, and the air escaped with a loud hiss. They looked around, but all remained quiet. Rex searched by the motorhome for a key under the bristly doormat and among the plastic pots containing wilted petunias. He lifted a loose paver and found one. He hesitated.

"This is unlawful entry. We're not even on home turf."

"If we don't act right away, we risk losing any hope of finding the girl. Her life could be at stake."

"Hand over John's baton, Alistair."

Rex fitted the key in the lock, with no idea of what they might find. The heavy door swung outwards, revealing a dark and chill interior, yet with a lived-in smell about it.

He switched on his torch and swept its light around the compactly furnished space strewn with items of men's clothing, RV magazines, and snack food wrappers. But no girl.

Alistair found another torch in the galley kitchen dividing the sleeping quarters from the seating area behind the cab. They located a coil of rope and a roll of duct tape under the sink, and a switchblade in a bedside drawer. A potential abductor's kit, Rex reflected, disappointed not to find more personal evidence that might connect the motorhome to Dan Sutter.

He was about to look through the clothes in the inbuilt, wood-veneer wardrobe at the back of the vehicle when he suddenly heard the scrunch of steps on the concrete slab outside the door. They simultaneously switched off their torches. Rex's heart slowed to a dull thud.

The door opened and a central light suddenly illuminated the interior. A skinny youth appeared at the entrance, startled to see Rex standing in the middle of the motorhome. Alistair, who had placed himself flat against the wall by the door grabbed him before he could run.

"Who are you?" his colleague asked, while Rex stepped forwards, closed the door, and barred it with his bulk.

"Who wants to know?"

"We do. That's why I asked."

Confronted by two big men in expensive coats, the newcomer visibly shrank. He was not tall to begin with, and was dressed in the manner of a teenage hip-hop wannabe commonly referred to as a chav, a newer breed of charmless and shiftless troublemakers. He wore a dark, sheeny Adidas zip-up jacket and matching sportswear tucked into his socks, along with trendy trainers and an earring, giving him a bad-boy look that Rex thought might appeal to teenage girls.

Despite his symmetrically appointed features, there was something shifty about him. He was carrying a plastic shopping bag, which he dangled beside his right leg and tried to hide from view.

"Justin Tims," he replied sullenly, twisting his head around at Rex. "I'm a warden here."

"Where are the owners?"

"In Minorca."

"What's there to do here?" Alistair enquired.

"Why? You blokes don't look like campers."

"Just answer the question."

"Crabbing, fishing. There's a shingly beach, an unheated outdoor pool, and a paddling pool for the kiddies. Oh yeah, and a skate park. You can walk to the town centre in ten minutes, where there's a social, pubs, shops, and a yacht club, if you're into booms and jigs," Tims added gamely. "I can let you rent a caravan for cheap. It's from the eighties, but in really good nick. It'll be vacant come Tuesday."

"What's in your bag?" Rex asked.

"Show us a badge."

"We're crown prosecutors, not the police." Rex repeated his question.

"Nuffink. Just beer and crisps, an' some DVDs, innit? Fancied a night in, like."

"What sort of DVDs?" Alistair grabbed the bag. "Disgusting," he expostulated as he pulled out the contents.

"You can talk, you old poofter."

Rex did not know what offended his friend most, being called old or a poofter, but Alistair's ire was instantaneous. He struck the lad in the mouth and gave him a split lip.

"I'm going to report you for that!" he wailed.

"When you're in possession of teen porn? I hardly think so."

Blood spurted from the young man's lip and streamed down his chin onto the white front of his tee-shirt. Alistair took out a handkerchief and fastidiously wiped off his fist even though he had been too quick to get blood on it.

"How old are you?" Rex demanded.

"You going to smack me in the gob if I don't answer?"

"I will," Alistair told him. "I'll split your top lip this time and you'll look like a duck."

"Twenty-nine."

Older than Rex had thought. "You might want to get some ice on that when we've finished with our questions."

Tims was using the bottom of his tee-shirt to blot the blood, exposing a pale, flaccid stomach, in spite of his skinny frame. Light brown fuzz around the belly button trailed down to his waistband. Feeling a vague revulsion, Rex pushed him further into the motorhome.

"What you going to do?" he squealed.

Rex pulled out a chair from the dinette. "Sit down. Is that your van parked outside?"

Tims sat. "Belongs to a camper. I let him use it 'cause my spot's bigger, innit?"

"I don't believe you."

"It's the truth. I wouldn't be seen dead driving a heap like that."

Rex stood over him. "Which camper?"

"He's renting the caravan I was telling you about. A white four-berth by the lake."

"What does he look like?"

"Nothing much. About fifty."

Rex and Alistair exchanged glances.

"He's staying there with his sister, though she looks a bit young to be his sister, if you know what I mean." The lad leered with his fat lip, on which the blood was beginning to clot.

His sister Amber? Rex thought at first, his mind turning to the woman in Wales; but she would hardly be young now. "A teenage girl went missing from Kent. She was abducted in a van similar to the one parked outside."

Tims' face, staring up at him, went completely white. "I told you, it's not mine!"

"What's the camper's name?"

"Dan."

"Dan what?"

"Can't remember! Mac somefink."

"McBride?"

Tims nodded. "Yeh, maybe."

"Is he there now?"

The young man shrugged.

"Whose caravan is it?"

"Nige and Sue's. They're the people wot run the place. Can you give us that ice? And some water?"

"Do you have a key to it?"

"I don't have a spare."

"Let's tie him up," Rex said, anxious to reconnoitre the caravan and see if the man and girl they were seeking were there. From his coat pocket he took the rope and bound Tim's wrists behind the chair-back.

"You can't leave me like this," their captive whined.

"Just while we see aboot your friend."

"He's not my friend."

"Accomplice then."

"He's not my—" Rex cut him off by placing a terry-cloth tea towel over his mouth and knotting it securely behind his ears; not that there was anyone around to hear him if he were able to cry out for help.

Alistair bound his ankles to the front legs of the chair. If he struggled, the rickety chair would topple over and he along with it.

The two men stepped down from the motorhome and shut the door.

"Do you think it was Lindsay Poulson he was talking about?" Alistair asked.

"I don't know."

They jogged across the open space towards the darkening lake, the ground uneven; damp and yielding in places, in others rutted and covered in loose stones. "We should have left Friday night and driven straight down," Rex gasped as he ran.

"You needed some sort of proof Sutter was here." Alistair's voice came out in laboured spurts.

Developing a stitch in his side, Rex caught his friend's arm and they slowed to a fast walk. He scoped out the handful of tents and unhitched caravans. One stood out, broadside to the lake, white with a grey stripe below its wide windows, and trapezium-shaped.

"That must be it," he rasped. "It's an older model caravan." He placed his hands over his knees while he regained his breath, praying the girl was still alive. He felt slightly nauseous.

"I don't know whether to hope it's her or not," Alistair said, voicing Rex's fears, his breath escaping in short foggy puffs. "What if we're too late?"

Rex summoned his calm and collected his thoughts. "Let's hope we're not. And if someone's there with her, at least we have the element of surprise."

THIRTY-FIVE

THE FLICKER OF A television behind the thin blue curtains betrayed occupancy. Rex had noticed an external TV aerial as he and Alistair half-circled the caravan from a safe distance before closing in slowly. Attached to the front above the hitch sat a large white plastic storage container with a metal lock. It looked sturdy enough to get up on, but the curtain in the window above was closely fitted and afforded no view inside.

They inspected the caravan from the lake side, where a sun-bleached awning stretched from the door over a picnic table on collapsible metal legs. Alistair picked it up and positioned it by the rectangular window at the back of the caravan. He tested the surface with his hands, bearing down on it.

Satisfied it could hold his weight, he clambered on top and knelt at the window, peering in through a gap above the top edge of the curtain. Rex watched him wobble and slide off the table in a hurry.

"There's a girl bound and gagged on a sofa-bed," he said in a hoarse whisper to Rex, who was watching the door.

"Lindsay?"

"Could be. It's dark except for the light from the TV. I could only see her silhouette. But it's definitely a young girl. I couldn't see anyone with her."

Alistair crept back to the window. Rex helped stabilize the table while his friend got up again. Alistair tapped gently on the window and mouthed a few words through the gap in the curtain.

"She's nodding her head. I think she's alone."

"How can you be sure?" Rex whispered back. "What if she's warning you?"

"I don't think so." Alistair asked, this time loud enough for Rex to hear, "Are you alone?" He glued his eye to the window. "She's nodding frantically now. We need to get in." He scrambled down from the table.

"What if she was being threatened by someone you couldn't see?"

"She seems quite composed, for someone who's tied up."

"Well, it's now or never, I suppose."

Rex pulled down on the door latch, not surprised to find it locked. A search for a key in all the obvious places revealed nothing. "What now?"

"I brought a crow bar under my coat."

"What crow bar?"

"From the motorhome. I'll pop out a window if need be."

Rex commended his friend's foresight, without fully comprehending how he had been able to run with a crowbar secreted in his coat, but now wasn't the time to ask. They tried all the windows Alistair could fit through, being the slimmer and more agile of the two, and found them locked too.

"It'll have to be the crowbar." Alistair selected the rear window and went to work while Rex kept a lookout.

He spotted a couple of shadows moving about on the far side of the lake, but they would not be able to see or hear what Alistair was up to at the back of the caravan. No one approached from the open ground whence they had come.

By dint of strength and perseverance, Alistair managed to get the window sufficiently open to flip it out all the way. He yanked it from its frame and set it down on the ground. Rex glanced nervously about him, worried about the noise, but focused on the girl.

Alistair drew the pleated curtain aside and called out softly, saying he was coming in and not to be afraid. He removed his bulky coat and threw it inside, and then hoisted himself through the opening and stepped into the caravan. His face reappeared briefly as he told Rex he would unlock the door for him.

The sound of the television was less muted inside. With the two men standing in the centre, the space was cramped, the padded vinyl ceiling barely clearing their heads. Rain began to patter on the dark skylight. An odour of damp rose from the carpet.

Rex found a light switch. The girl sat to his left on one of two sofa-beds attached to the front side walls. Her hair was shiny and brushed, her blue eyes stretched wide above the gag. He could not remember what colour Lindsay's eyes were supposed to be. She wore a grey jersey tracksuit with purple stripes down the sleeves and legs, and socks and slippers on her bound feet.

He undid both the gag and the cotton scarf around her wrists, which was tied loosely enough to not be uncomfortable and yet tightly enough to be secure. Her hands trembled in her lap. He now clearly recognized her as the girl he had seen on the news in recent weeks, down to the dark mole on her cheekbone.

"Where is he, Lindsay?" he asked as Alistair took up the TV remote on the wood table separating the beds and switched off the set.

"The pub, I think. He comes back smelling of beer." She was nicely spoken and quiet in her demeanour.

"What's his name?"

"Danny. That's all I know."

They would have to leave it to the police to search the caravan for further identification. "You're a very brave girl," Rex said. "We're here to help you."

Only then did she begin to cry, huge tears welling in her eyes.

"How long is he usually gone for?" He attempted to keep the urgency out of his voice, but his first concern was to get her to safety before her abductor returned.

"Usually not much more than an hour. He left three-quarters of an hour ago," she said glancing at a clock embedded between two in-built lockers above the front window.

All the cupboards and drawers were in the same medium-toned wood, the place tidier than the motorhome, Rex noted in passing. "Did he harm you?"

She shook her head. "Not really. He brings me clothes and magazines, cakes, sweets … I pretend to like everything. He said I was a good girl, not like the one he took in Edinburgh, who screamed and struggled and made him so angry he had to … " She gulped. "Silence her."

Everything seemed to slow down for a brief moment in time. The terrified girl, the wood-clad surroundings, the white clock face, the raindrops plinking on the roof. Rex snapped to and instructed Alistair to call DCI Lauper's contact in Colchester.

His friend paced the few steps to the back of the caravan as he spoke on the phone. A white curtain, used to partition off the two pairs of beds, was draped to one side. The girl bent over her knees to unbind her ankles, her silky brown hair sweeping forward as she did so.

"Have you been here the entire time?"

She nodded fearfully. "He only ever let me out to use the showers. He took me out at night with my hands tied and, once inside, there was no way to escape." Her voice came out muffled as she attended to the task of freeing her feet. She sat up, her face flushed, and pushed her hair back behind her shoulders, pausing as she did so. "He brushes my hair and calls me Amber. It's dead creepy."

"His father mistreated his sister," Rex said. "He may in his own mind be trying to make amends, but he's dangerous and unpredictable. We need to get you away. You can call your parents from the car."

The girl flinched at the mention of a car.

"It's okay. We're advocates," Alistair told her, returning his phone to his coat pocket.

"What's that?"

"Scottish barristers," Rex explained. "We prosecute criminals. Anything you need from here?"

"My schoolbag."

"Any luck with the local police?" he asked Alistair.

"On their way, but we should get out of here. Do you have a jacket?" he asked Lindsay.

She opened a wardrobe and extracted a crimson blazer, which she hastened to put on over her tracksuit. She pulled out a black leather book bag and strapped it to her shoulders. She was still wearing slippers.

"Where are your shoes?" Rex asked.

"I don't know. They're not in here."

"Never mind."

They filed out of the caravan into the rain, Alistair leading the way and Rex closing the rear. Night had all but fallen and pinpricks of light dotted the campsite, but nobody stirred. He picked Lindsay up in his arms and ran after Alistair across the soggy grass. The girl weighed little enough, but jogging with her in his heavy coat provided him with an unaccustomed work-out on top of his earlier sprint to the lake.

When they reached the Jaguar, he put her down thankfully, and she clambered into the back seat. He shrugged out of the coat and got in beside Alistair, his throat tight and parched and his heart thumping fast.

THIRTY-SIX

As they drove off, Lindsay broke into tears of relief. Rex passed her a roll of paper towels from under his seat, and she tore off a wad and blotted her hair dry. Alistair turned up the heat in the car and she removed her damp blazer. Something fluttered from her sleeve.

She picked it up, clearly not wishing to litter Alistair's immaculate interior.

"Is that a stamp hinge?" Rex held out his palm and carefully placed it in his wallet.

"It was caught in the cuff of my sleeve."

"Those pesky little hinges." Alistair glanced round with a smile.

"He has an album with stamps from different countries, which he'd let me look at. They reminded me there was a world outside the caravan and made me think I might never get to see any of those places."

"Now you will," said Alistair.

Rex surmised that if Sutter had the album, he had probably taken the other items as well. "What sort of watch does he wear?" he asked

Lindsay, checking his own, amazed to see how little time had passed since they had left the Masthead, in spite of all the ensuing action.

"A gold-plated one with a stretchy gold bracelet. Why?"

"A watch and stamp album went missing from a house in Canterbury."

"He did more than burgle the house, didn't he?"

"Perhaps."

"He killed that girl in Edinburgh." She began to cry again.

"Tell me, Lindsay, did he say anything else on the subject of the other girl?"

"Only that he forced her into his car as she was walking home from school and took her to his basement flat. He had to get rid of her, he said, because she wouldn't be quiet and do what she was told, and he dumped her body in a dark alley."

"Skinner's Close. It made national headline news, but you'd have been too young at the time to remember."

Alistair turned onto Victoria Place where the buildings and shopfronts glistened and the lights showed blurry in the rain. They had not gone far along the road leading out of town when a lone police car sped by in the opposite direction, tyres swishing on the wet tar and siren wailing. Alistair slowed down.

"Keep going, please don't stop," Lindsay urged in a strangled voice from the back seat. "I just want to get far away from here."

Alistair kept going.

"He took my phone. I need to ring my mum," she pleaded.

Alistair gave her his mobile while Rex called the police on his to explain that they had rescued Lindsay Poulson from the campsite in Brightlingsea and her abductor, Dan Sutter, was possibly in one of the local pubs. While Lindsay spoke to her parents, alternately crying and reassuring them, he told the dispatcher where exactly the caravan and repainted van were located, in case the police car they had passed had not been responding to their emergency after Alistair's call.

They parked in a layby and waited in the event Sutter tried to leave in the van by the main road out of town. After an emotional exchange with her younger sister Christie, Lindsay passed the phone back to Alistair and wiped her teary face with her sleeve.

"Dan Sutter can't have been here all the time," Rex said to her. "He was in Edinburgh two weeks ago." At Pruitt's flat.

"The first Sunday, he left for two days. An elderly woman came to guard me. She had a Scottish accent too. She didn't say much. She brought me a pork pie and heated up some baked beans on the gas hob. The rest of the time it was just toast and Marmite. She never took me to the communal facilities, and I had to use the porta potty. She said if I tried to escape it would mean trouble for me, and for her."

"I have some bottled water and date bars if you're hungry," Alistair said, glancing into his rear view mirror. "We had no idea we'd find you; we came looking for Sutter on another matter, so I'm afraid we came ill-prepared."

"I'm not hungry, thank you. I just want to go home."

"I know, and you will soon," Rex promised her.

He imagined her family rejoicing back in Dover, and yet anxious to see her and make sure she was all right. He could still scarcely believe that she was safe. Pale and no doubt more traumatized than she let show, but not physically hurt, it appeared.

"Did you happen to notice if he kept a spare tyre in the van?" he asked.

"There was one in the back. I've never been so terrified in my life. I kept thinking the police were bound to find me because some-one must have spotted his ugly brown van."

"Two witnesses came forward, but he whitewashed it."

She took a deep breath. "What if he gets away?"

"Unlikely," Rex assured her, twisting around in the front passenger seat to face her. "We sabotaged his van."

She responded with the shadow of a smile, the first.

It would take a while for Sutter to change his tyre once he discovered it was flat. First he would go searching the campsite for Lindsay, imagining perhaps that she had managed to get free on her own. On the other hand, he might borrow or steal a car.

"What should we do aboot the wee creep in the motorhome?" he suddenly asked Alistair, having forgotten about him in the excitement of saving Lindsay.

"Let the police find him and his stash of illegal DVDs."

"Aye, let him stew for a bit. Did a young man by the name of Justin Tims have anything to do with your abduction, Lindsay?"

"No, it was just Danny and the woman."

"His mother, I believe. How did he snatch you? Take your time; he can't get to you now."

She blew her nose noisily. Rex and Alistair exchanged paternal smiles, relishing the calm before the storm. There would be the police and an onslaught of publicity to contend with soon enough.

"I was walking home from school, just like the other girl," Lindsay began. "He was parked by the pavement. There was a brick wall on my other side. He was opening the back doors of the van when I went by. I didn't think much of it. I was on my phone. He grabbed me, ripped it from my hand, and bundled me inside. There were no windows in the back compartment, just a pile of mouldy old blankets. When I realized I couldn't get out, I started to cry. He told me he wouldn't hurt me if I was good and didn't try to escape. He said he was protecting me."

"From what?" Rex asked.

"My father, he told me later. I don't know why. My father's never done anything wrong in his life! I don't think that man Danny is all there."

A swarm of squad cars with flashing roof lights converged at the turning to Brightlingsea and set up a road block. Rex got out. The rain had stopped and a sliver of moon glimmered ethereally in the murky sky, reflected in puddles on the road.

He informed the first officer he came upon that Lindsay Poulson was in his colleague's car and not in need of immediate medical attention as far as he could tell.

He prepared himself for the inevitable series of questions and statements at the police station, only too happy to comply. His only concern was that, in spite of what he had told Lindsay, Dan Sutter might still escape.

THIRTY-SEVEN

WHILE GIVING THEIR STATEMENTS at the station, Rex and Alistair learned that Sutter had been spotted by a helicopter sent in to conduct a sweep of Brightlingsea. Fleeing on foot, he had reached the housing estate on the inland side of town and had ducked out of sight.

An hour later, a police dog tracked him to a garden shed where, heavily outnumbered and surrounded by a tactical support unit, he had been smoked out and had resisted arrest. The shed belonged to his great aunt, who had not appeared unduly concerned when he was taken into custody. His mother had already left on the bus to the train station, apparently to return to her post in Canterbury.

It transpired that Annie planned to take care of her aunt on the understanding she would inherit the house when she died. Aunt Fifi made it clear to police that she did not approve of her great nephew's criminal record and had refused to let him stay with her, and so he rented a caravan at the campsite.

Rex wondered what would have happened to Lindsay by Tuesday, when Tims had said Sutter was vacating it. Moving her to another place would have been risky. He had already kept her for over two weeks. Rex did not fancy her chances, considering what had happened to April Showers.

Now headed back to Canterbury, he sank into the padded seat while Alistair drove. He found himself squinting in the glare of oncoming headlights and closed his heavy lids. Lindsay was on her way back to Kent to be reunited with her parents and sister, who were driving out to meet her halfway. Alistair had put on the seat warmers, and Rex felt the length of his spine finally begin to relax after sitting in an uncomfortable chair at the station for what had seemed like ages.

His friend set some classical music on low, as though anticipating Rex's desire to think events through. And think he did as they regained the A12.

The private investigator had said Sutter senior had died in a homeless shelter two months before, from liver complications. Dan's sister had left home at fifteen. That left his mother, who had unaccountably agreed to keep Lindsay captive. Annie might be an elderly woman, but Rex felt little compassion.

He called Phoebe and asked whether she had returned yet.

"I don't think so. I've been upstairs working on some new curtains to keep my mind off things. Did you find him?"

"Aye, he's been holed up at a campsite in Brightlingsea. Annie's been staying at her aunt's house there. Did you not see the news?"

"No, why?"

"Sutter is the man who snatched Lindsay Poulson from Dover."

Phoebe gave a small scream. "Are you sure?"

"We found the girl in his caravan. I think he might have been thinking of fleeing to France but could not resist another abduction before leaving our shores."

"Another abduction?"

"Lindsay told us he had taken another girl, in Edinburgh. I'm almost certain it was April Showers."

"So Richard Pruitt was right about him. Oh my goodness, this is a lot to take in, Rex. Are you still in Essex?"

"We're approaching the Dartford Tunnel and then we're going straight to Canterbury Station to meet Annie off the train. If it's the one we think she's on, we might just make it. Ring me if she turns up in the meantime, and just pretend you don't know anything. Can you do that?"

"I'll try. I think I need a stiff drink."

Rex hoped Phoebe would stick to only one and not make it too stiff. She needed to keep her wits about her. As did they.

THIRTY-EIGHT

THE TRAIN WAS JUST pulling into the station when Rex and Alistair arrived. Fortunately for them, it had been delayed. However, their plan to intercept Annie before she returned to St. Dunstan's Terrace depended on her not having been warned of her son's arrest and taking off somewhere else.

Alistair left the car illegally parked close to the station entrance and they went to meet the incoming trickle of passengers from the platform. Annie was not among them. And then, just as Rex was about to turn away, he spied her at the back, wearing a headscarf and tweed coat and pulling a small suitcase on wheels. She looked surprised but not panicked to see him.

"Can we give you a lift home?" he asked. "This is my friend and colleague, Alistair Frazer. He has his car right outside."

He took her suitcase before she could object, and Alistair escorted her to the Jaguar and opened the front passenger door. She seemed amazed to be riding in such splendour and unaware of events unfolding back in Brightlingsea. Apparently, no one had contacted her.

Rex got in the back, well pleased to have Annie McBride in his grasp. He wished to have a few words with her before he turned her over to Kent Police, who worked closely with the Essex force. He asked after her daughter and grandchildren as they drove the short distance to Phoebe's house.

"Grand," she said, and added that she had enjoyed a nice quiet weekend with them.

Alistair said he was an old acquaintance of Mrs. Wells' and explained that he and Rex were staying overnight on a brief business trip.

"It's nice she has a bit o' company," Annie commented.

They pulled up in front of the house and Alistair hastened around the bonnet to open the car door for her while Rex retrieved her suitcase. While Annie let herself into the house, Alistair gave Rex a conspiratorial wink. They followed her into the hall as Phoebe was descending the staircase.

"Ah, I see you have all returned safely," she declared with a natural smile.

"These gentlemen gave me a lift from the station," Annie said, as though edified by the experience and not at all puzzled by the fact they had just happened to be there.

Rex offered to take her suitcase downstairs and did so without waiting for a response. "I don't know aboot you, Annie, but I fancy a cup of tea." He filled the kettle at the sink.

"Och, let me make it," Annie said, removing her coat.

He let her prepare the tea and then invited her to sit down at the kitchen table, saying he had a few questions and requesting her co-operation. She did so submissively, her face betraying no anxiety, nor even much curiosity.

"The questions relate to your son."

She glanced up from her mug of tea, her face finally registering shock. She had never mentioned her son to Phoebe and now clearly wondered what was afoot.

Rex set his phone to record and placed it between them. "I came here to informally assist Mrs. Wells in a case involving some missing items and other suspicious circumstances surrounding her father's death. My inquiry led me to Dan."

"Danny never killed the old man," Annie insisted without prevarication. "He had a heart attack when he saw him. The judge sent him down for ten years. Ten long years! It broke him."

"And where were you at the time of the judge's death, Annie?"

"At the cinema wi' a friend," she replied, sounding rehearsed.

"I know that's not true," Rex gambled. The waddle under her chin trembled. "You were waiting by the gate on New Street, were you not?"

"Aye."

"To make sure no one saw your son enter the house by the window."

She nodded, her throat wobbling in earnest.

"Please answer for the recording."

She glanced nervously at Rex's phone. "Aye, I did."

The answers were coming more easily than Rex could have hoped. She made no effort to defend herself, perhaps because she was accustomed to succumbing to someone else's control.

"And you must have left the upstairs window unlatched before you left for the evening, ostensibly to go to the cinema. A random housebreaker would not have known the window would be unlocked."

Annie gazed at him with the frightened, vacant stare of a rabbit.

"You planted the hair clasp and glove fragment in Judge Murgatroyd's room to throw me off the scent. You used your employer's

195

nail varnish to further mislead me and perhaps even to implicate Mrs. Wells and make it look like she had made everything up."

No response from the housekeeper, but no denial either.

"Your son is in serious trouble, Annie, maybe more than you know. I just came from Brightlingsea."

"He never meant to hurt the lass. I have nothing more to say. He's my son and he's all I have left."

"I'm sorry, Annie, truly I am, but he's broken numerous laws and I doubt he'll ever leave prison again."

Annie continued to look at him blankly, but her knotty hands shook and she placed them below the table.

"I fail to understand how you could assist your son in his intention to murder an old man and how you could condone his kidnapping of a schoolgirl and holding her prisoner. Her parents have been going out of their minds these past weeks. Did you not once give them a thought?"

"Danny took good care of the girl. He never meant her any harm."

Rex grit his teeth. "So you keep saying. You betrayed Mrs. Wells' trust, helped precipitate the judge's death, and aided and abetted in the false imprisonment of a minor. I believe you also warned your son that I would be visiting Richard Pruitt at his flat, and that's how he came to be there. You had seen correspondence from Pruitt to Judge Murgatroyd. Pruitt's is a name your son would know very well, since he was charged in Dan's stead for April Showers' murder. Your son attempted to kill him to keep him quiet. Were you aware of that? And he attacked me and my friend Alistair!"

Rex stopped himself before he lost control of his temper. He pushed his tea away. "Ann McBride, I'm placing you under citizen's arrest."

Her expression remained impassive and she did not move a muscle in her chair. Rex made sure the door to the back garden was locked and he put the key in his pocket. He further ensured that the elderly woman could not escape by any other exit.

"Unlikely you'll be spending another night under this roof," he told her as he was leaving the kitchen to go back upstairs. "I suggest you pack up your things promptly."

How long she had known her son was guilty of April Showers' murder was something the police could ascertain. Thanks to Lindsay's testimony, however, Dan Sutter could now be legitimately linked to that case.

"You'll have to manage without Annie from now on," he announced to Phoebe upon entering the living room.

"Did you get a confession?" Alistair asked from where he sat in an armchair, a tumbler of whisky in hand.

"She admitted to watching her son break into the house. I suggest we give young Constable Bryant's career a boost. Phoebe, can you see if he's on duty and have him come over? He can take Annie in as an accomplice in the housebreaking and in Lindsay's imprisonment."

While Phoebe telephoned the station, Rex helped himself to two thimblefuls of Glenlivet.

"PC Bryant is on his way," she reported minutes later, sitting back down and folding her hands in her lap in an attitude of anticipation. "What else did Annie say?"

Rex stepped into the hall and listened out for any sounds from the basement. Satisfied Annie had not stirred from her quarters he returned to the living room.

"Not only did she stand guard by the gate, but she had taken care to unlock your father's window before leaving for her night off. She says her son did not actually murder him. Seeing Dan Sutter by his bedside might have been enough to cause a heart attack."

"Is that all she told you?"

"Aye, but we know she was with Lindsay Poulson while her son was in Edinburgh, and that he took your father's watch and album, which Lindsay described. The stamp collection held nothing of real value, as originally supposed. It was just lying on your father's desk, and he presumably took it as a memento, perhaps hoping it might fetch something."

"Annie took an active part." Phoebe sank back into the sofa cushions and shook her head in disbelief. Then she scowled. "That woman knew everything and played me along from the start!"

"From the moment she applied for the position of housekeeper, it seems, and inserted herself unobtrusively into your household. It can't be a coincidence she ended up here. She and Sutter must have plotted revenge while he was still in prison."

"But I go by Mrs. Wells. How would she have known I was Gordon Murgatroyd's daughter or that he was living with me? Oh, wait a minute." Phoebe made a grimace. "I said in the advertisement that the position would entail helping take care of a retired judge. I thought it would reassure applicants that they would be working in a respectable household."

"Perhaps she saw the word 'judge' and made some enquiries."

"She was at my father's funeral! The hypocrisy of the woman!"

"She denies her son's direct culpability in your father's death, of course, but it's highly probable he's responsible for mugging your elderly neighbour in a case of mistaken identity." Rex paced methodically between Phoebe and Alistair as he spoke.

"Annie told her son of my impending visit to Richard Pruitt's flat. Remember our discussing that while she was serving us dinner, Phoebe? Sutter cut his throat before he could voice his suspicions to me regarding Sutter's involvement in the April Showers murder. Then, after Annie heard from our telephone conversation that Richard was still alive, she planted a few red herrings in your father's room to make it look like a woman had broken in."

Phoebe's face remained stony. "To think she was spying on me the whole time!"

"And frustrating your attempts to get to the bottom of your father's death," Alistair added.

"Indeed. What about Dad's wig?" Phoebe asked Rex.

"We found one similar in Richard's attic. Now that we know Sutter stole the stamp album and watch from here, it's apparent he took the wig as well, and left it in the spot where Richard kept a shoebox containing information on him as a warning not to meddle. I'm just not sure when he put it there, since the police have not got back to me yet regarding what was on the CCTV tapes. Alistair said Sutter wasn't carrying a box when he left the flat after his attack on Richard."

"That's right," Alistair confirmed. "Possibly he came back to continue his search when Richard was in hospital and left the wig for you before taking off. A 'pursue this investigation and you'll be dead, too' sort of thing."

"Can we prove he was instrumental in my father's death?"

"Perhaps a second opinion can be sought as to whether your father died of a heart attack or else was asphyxiated," Rex said. "If such can be proved." Though he sincerely hoped Phoebe would not have the judge's grave disturbed.

"Scared to death or smothered by a pillow; either way, Sutter is responsible," Phoebe declared. "At least now we can prove he was here."

"Just think," Alistair addressed Phoebe. "If you hadn't opened up the investigation, Lindsay Poulson may never have been found. So your father's death was by no means in vain."

Phoebe looked thoughtful for a moment. "That's very true," she acknowledged.

Dan Sutter had a lot to answer for, Rex reflected with anger. The Showers had lost their own daughter forever. Adding to their misery, Stu had caught his hand in a machine at work while still reeling from his grief, and as a result had lost his job. The benefits he received were poor compensation for limited use of a hand. Rex hoped he would derive some peace in knowing the truth at last.

"After a good deal of thought, I've decided to put the house on the market," Phoebe announced, interrupting his thoughts. "It's not the same without Doug or Dad, and it's time to downsize. I want to move back to Edinburgh and reconnect with old friends. And both of you, of course," she said with a smile.

"I'll host a welcome home party for you," Alistair offered, raising his tumbler.

The doorbell rang at that moment.

"That'll be Constable Bryant," Phoebe said, getting up from the sofa.

"It's turning into a very long night," Rex said to Alistair, suppressing a yawn. "We won't get much sleep."

"I cleared it with Smiley while you were downstairs talking to the felonious housekeeper," Alistair informed him. "We don't have to get back to the grindstone until Tuesday."

"So Smiley's not going to lecture us aboot taking the law into our own hands?"

"Well, he might have to smooth some ruffled feathers on our behalf, but he's still giving us the day off."

In that case, Rex thought happily, they could stop over in Derby on the way back to Edinburgh the following day and see Helen. He had something important to tell her.

THIRTY-NINE

"THE CONQUERING HEROES HAVE returned!" Helen exclaimed, welcoming Rex and Alistair back into her home. "It's all over the news. Lindsay Poulson safe and sound and reunited with her family! Tears of joy! And on the TV they showed footage of the helicopter flying low over Brightlingsea, searchlights blazing, and Sutter from the air evading arrest. It was riveting!"

She stopped when she saw the men's blasé expressions. "Celebrity not to your liking?" she asked as she took their coats.

"Not so much," Rex replied. "It seems reporters are turning up at our homes and besieging our place of work. They didn't waste much time. Mother tells me Miss Bird is shooing them off the doorstep with her broom."

"Your mother must be so proud of you, as am I. I suppose you could go about incognito but you're a hard person to disguise."

Alistair laughed. "Only Richard Pruitt is enjoying the attention now that Sutter's been caught and is no longer a threat. He's been vindicated."

"Judge Murgatroyd saw that Richard might be innocent," Rex said. "It's almost as though he were still presiding." All threads led back to the judge, Rex remembered from his dream. "Justice has ultimately been served."

"Good old Judge M," Alistair cheered. "The contrary old so-and-so!"

"But what about the poor girl?" Helen asked, leading them into the sitting room where a tea tray awaited. "She must have been in a terrible state when you found her."

"She'd been well enough cared for, I think." Rex sat beside his fiancée on the sofa. "She was frightened and tearful, but I don't think it had all sunk in yet. I'm sure the floodgates fully opened when she was back in her family's arms."

"She's a remarkable young girl," Alistair added. "I'm convinced she had a lot to do with the fact she's still alive. She instinctively knew not to antagonize her captor and to play along with his sister fantasy."

"I don't think he would ever have stopped acting out that fantasy for as long as he was a free man," Helen opined.

While Alistair went off to make a phone call, Rex pulled her closer and took her hands in his.

"I've been meaning to say this for a while," he began. "I want to spend more time with you." Helen opened her mouth to speak, but he continued to say what had been in his heart and on his mind. "I've been considering chucking in my day job and working on private cases full time. It would entail a certain amount of travelling, and I'd still have to take care of Mother, but I could move here, if that's what you want."

Helen stared at him in surprise. "Rex, no. Absolutely not! I've been giving us some thought too. I'm ready to make the move. Things are changing at the school. It's become more political and, well, perfectly petty! Especially compared to what you and Alistair have been through."

"Are you sure? I know it's asking a lot."

"It's what I want," Helen assured him.

"To marry me and move to Edinburgh?" Rex asked, just to be sure.

"Yes, silly."

Rex let out an elated breath. "We can take over the whole of my floor at the Morningside house and spend more time at Gleneagle Lodge. How does that sound?"

Helen smiled at him tenderly. "It sounds perfect." She leaned in and placed her lips on his, sealing her words with a kiss.